Head Count

By

Janet Taylor-Perry

Head Count

Janet Taylor-Perry

A Laura Beth Copeland Misadventure #1

Dragon Breath Press
Ridgeland, MS

ISBN: 978-0-9990692-4-0

Other Books by Janet Taylor-Perry

The Raiford Chronicles:

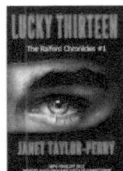   

Lucky Thirteen
http://amzn.to/1ld8grm
Heartless
http://amzn.to/1iWuYmP
Broken
http://goo.gl/6YTwyz
Whatever It Takes
http://goo.gl/1eLv66
The Legend of Draconis:

King Satin's Realm
http://goo.gl/wf7UbM
Spirits' Desire
Winner: Preditors and Editors Award
2017, Best "Other" Novel

goo.gl/H9St2K

April Chastain Intrigues:

Wilted Magnolias
https://goo.gl/2oJOjc
Hillbilly Hijinks

https://www.amazon.com/dp/0999069233
Homegrown Healer

Dedication

For Betty Maugh (O'Brien), my high school journalism and creative writing teacher. You encouraged me to follow my dreams and use my gifts. It has taken me a long time to do that, but your influence has always been in my heart. You were the first real flowerchild that I ever met. You were a free spirit. I have been called that over the years. Perhaps, your spirit touched mine, as the dragons' spirits touch their bonded humans in my stories in *The Legend of Draconis*. I remember what you wrote in my senior memories book. You said I reminded you of a Kung Fu meditation. "He who knows others is wise. He who knows himself is enlightened." Well, I lost myself for a while, but in writing the Draconis series, I have once again found myself, and your words constantly come to mind as I pen new stories. Thank you for helping me not to completely lose sight of who I am.

Take a census of the whole Israelite community by their clans and families, listing every man by name, one by one.

Numbers 1:2

Acknowledgements

As always, I must thank my friend, mentor and editor, Lottie Brent Boggan for continuing to push me to hone my writing skills. She can be brutal! Lottie is also an author, and her books are available on Amazon. Look for her next release—*Return to Redemption Ridge*, the long-awaited sequel to her award-winning novel, *Redemption Ridge*, coming soon.

Great appreciation also goes to The Red Dog Writers who sat through weeks of Friday meetings and listened to this story in its infancy, as well as my friends at thenextbigwriter.com who read this in 2011 and offered much needed critique.

Again, my cover is made possible by my awesome former student, Christopher Chambers. You can contact him at juroddesigns.com.

I suppose I should offer some form of acknowledgement to the U.S. Census Bureau for the experience of working the 2010 census and having a woman slam her door in my face. When I went back to try to interview her again, she would not open the door, but I saw her feet through the miniblinds and wondered what she had to hide. Thus, my imagination began to run wild, so my census enumerator saw a decapitated head rather than feet. Thereupon, Laura Beth Copeland was born.

Contents

Dedication

Cameras flashed and reporters shouted as men in black suits escorted the witness into the courthouse, shielding her from prying eyes. Once inside, she was ushered into a small room to wait. Mid-morning, the bailiff opened the door. "It's your turn, ma'am."

The woman took the stand and met the eyes of the accused. As if loosening his tie, the man discreetly ran a finger across his neck, indicating the witness's imminent demise if she opened her mouth. His eyes bored into hers and she trembled under his gaze.

Her hand shook perceptively when she placed it on the Bible. The lady sat once she swore to tell the truth. The prosecutor approached. "Mrs. Perez, first tell the court if you're testifying today in exchange for anything."

"Yes, my life."

"Has the prosecution coerced you in any way?"

"No. I'm testifying so I can escape the monster I married."

Testimony continued in the case of Carlos Antonio Perez, one of America's most connected drug lords with a Mexican cartel, for the next week. Five witnesses and one undercover FBI agent whose identity was kept secret presented damning evidence.

The verdict returned—Guilty on all counts.

Along with four others, Consuela Garcia-Perez disappeared.

1
Temporary Work

Laura Beth Copeland, a stay-home mother of two and a half, sat in the training session, listening intently as the instructor explained how to conduct an "in-mover" enumerator questionnaire, EQ for short, for the census bureau. "I don't understand," said an older woman who sat beside her.

The younger woman replied to her fellow soon-to-be census-taker, "It's simple, Madeleine. An in-mover is a person who has moved into the residence since April first. If the person says they filed a census questionnaire at their previous address, write down that address and the person's name and move on. If they didn't, complete an EQ for their *former* address."

"Why don't they say it like that then? It's all about where you lived on April Fool's Day." With a slight grin, Madeleine looked at the younger woman who was already showing that she was expecting a child. There was nothing intimidating about the petite redhead with big brown eyes, but the way she spoke showed she could hold her own in any situation. Madeleine asked, "Why are you doing this? You don't need the money. Your husband's a doctor."

"I thought it'd be interesting, and I'd meet different kinds of people. Why are you doing it?"

"I need the money. It's hard living on a fixed income. Pension and social security just aren't enough. How are you going to walk around to houses in your condition?"

"My condition? I'm not sick. I'm having a baby."

The instructor suddenly said, "Mrs. Copeland, will you come and demonstrate this scenario with me?"

Laura Beth performed the role-playing situation of an in-mover interview with the instructor admirably and returned to her seat beside Madeleine. When the group broke for lunch, she invited the older woman to join her, and they stopped in the nearby Western Sizzlin' to eat. Laura Beth insisted lunch was her treat. She realized the older widow who lived alone with her two cats did not have funds to dine out.

Over lunch the two women chatted. Madeleine asked, "How long have you been married to my doctor?"

"*Your* doctor? You've seen Bruce? But he's an oncologist."

Madeleine nodded. "Lymphoma. Cancer free for three years now. Having him here made life easier than having to drive all the way to Jackson and University Medical Center. Not too many doctors would set up a satellite clinic like he did."

"He's one in a million," Laura Beth agreed. "I'm glad he was able to help you. We've been married seven years. We have two children, Stacey, five, and Tonya, three. This one is a boy, due September twelfth, and probably the last." She patted her tummy. "We're still discussing names. Tell me about your husband."

"William and I were married almost forty years. He passed away with a major coronary three days before our anniversary." She squeezed lemon into her tea. "We have three boys who live all over the country."

"Are you close to them?"

"We talk on the phone. They were glad I sold our big old house."

"Well, the garden home address you have is in a nice, safe neighborhood. Did you work before?"

"Yes, I was a teacher for thirty years."

"Here?"

"The high school. I taught any form of science you can name, and I coached the girls' basketball team to three state titles." Madeleine drank a swig of tea. "You're not from here?"

"No, I grew up on the Gulf Coast, but I like it here. I still think Sunrise, Mississippi, is an amusing name for a town, but it's a pleasant place to raise a family. The Delta is so different from the Gulf Coast."

Madeleine laughed. "Mississippi has a lot of funny little town names."

"Yeah, I've been through Hot Coffee and Cold Water." She raised her glass of ice water and drank a mock toast. "Actually, Bruce grew up near Hot Coffee in Taylorsville, another small town."

"Mississippi is chock full of small towns. That's one reason it's so important to count all the people. We can't afford to lose representation in Congress." The older woman ate some of the baked chicken on her plate. "We lost a representative in the 2000 census because our population declined. God only knows how low it might be after Katrina."

"True. Sunrise is large compared to places that you'd miss if you blinked. I'm betting we come out to have about thirteen thousand folks." They finished their meal before Laura Beth said, "Let's get back. We test this afternoon after a couple of hours on the streets."

"You'll do fine. Just don't overdo in your non-sick condition."

The women laughed and returned to training to pick up a binder of addresses that needed to be canvassed. Madeleine started in her own neighborhood, and Laura Beth picked up an apartment complex.

~

Laura Beth knocked on several doors, leaving notices-of-visit at most places when no one answered her summons. She completed one questionnaire with three household members and another in which the woman joked about not being able to claim her dog. At the next apartment, Laura Beth encountered a woman who seemed nervous. The woman said, "No, I didn't live here on that date. I just moved in. As a matter of fact, I'm still unpacking boxes."

"May I ask if you completed a census questionnaire at your former address?"

"I really don't want to talk about my former address. I need you to leave."

"Oh, can I have your name, please, as the respondent and a phone number where my supervisor could reach you if he needs to?"

"Maria Biaggi. No, you can't have a phone number."

The in-mover went inside and closed the door with a measure of force. Laura Beth left, feeling unsettled about the encounter. She had not expected any such resistance to being counted.

She returned to the final training session where they discussed their experiences and shared what to do in different situations. Laura Beth turned in her completed questionnaires, including the in-mover who had refused to answer questions regarding her previous address. The new census-takers took their tests, and the supervisor handed them to Madeleine to score while he looked over the completed questionnaires. The tall, older man with aristocratic Native American looking facial structure, Doug Blanchard, the supervisor, winked at Madeleine. Laura Beth grinned at the exchange. The group was dismissed and told to report back to the same location every evening after six but before eight so that completed questionnaires could be collected and time and travel forms could be completed.

On Saturday, Laura Beth visited every address in her binder that she had not visited the previous day and completed half her questionnaires. When she came to turn in her work and time sheet, Blanchard handed her the in-mover questionnaire. "I read your notes, but the local office will return this if you don't try again. Go back by in a couple of days. Maybe the woman was just harried because she was moving in. The other two are fine.

Good work." He signed off on her time sheet and took her surveys.

Laura Beth took Sunday off as a matter of principle. When the teenager she used as a babysitter came at four on Monday, Laura Beth went back to addresses where she had left notices-of-visit. She completed half a dozen more polls before seven and decided to hit one more before turning in her work for the day.

Thinking a whole weekend would have given her in-mover plenty of time to unpack, Laura Beth knocked on her door again. The sun was getting low, but she still had time to complete the questionnaire and get to the meeting place. She waited a moment and knocked a second time. Her eye caught something in the slightly-cracked Venetian blind. She shook her head and leaned in closer to the window.

Laura Beth Copeland's shriek reverberated through the apartment complex. She dropped every EQ she had. Her breath came in sharp gasps. Her hands fluttered as she fumbled with the catch on her fanny pack and pulled out her cell phone, dialing 9-1-1.

A black Escalade with tinted windows screeched tires as it peeled out from the parking area in front of the building. Laura Beth sank to the concrete by the door, unable to move.

2
One Potato, Two Potato, Three Potato, Four

Four Sunrise Police cruisers wailed through the apartment complex, leaving the stink of burning rubber behind them as they skidded to a halt. Officers sprang from their cars and rushed to the red-haired woman who sat on the concrete. Getting out of an unmarked car, a tall Nordic-looking man in a navy-blue suit knelt beside her. "Ma'am, I'm Detective Sergeant McGill. Can you tell me what happened? Where's the body?"

Laura Beth pointed, still feeling short of breath. "A head. There's a head in there. I didn't see the rest of the body."

"Are you sure, ma'am?"

She nodded. "I tried to interview her Friday for the census. It's the same lady. She said her name was Maria Biaggi."

Detective McGill stood and looked through the cracked blind. "Holy shit!" He began to signal to seal off the complex. "Ma'am did you see anyone leaving?"

"No." She shook her head. "A black SUV sped out as I called you."

"Tag number?"

"No." She looked up. "I'm sorry. I was a little preoccupied with calling the cops."

"So, you didn't see the driver?"

"No."

A tall, blonde female officer walked up. "Boss, both exits to the complex have been blocked."

The man nodded. "We might be looking for a black SUV, Dixon."

"Can you be more specific, Boss?"

"Nope, not yet. Officer Dixon, would you take care of our witness? Get her away from here. We have to get inside." He offered his hand to Laura Beth. "What's your name, ma'am?"

Laura Beth held tightly to the detective's arm. She still felt wobbly. "Thanks. I'm Laura Beth Copeland." She showed him her census I.D. and then looked around her. "Will you help me gather these forms? I have to call my supervisor since the confidentiality of the questionnaires might have been compromised. He'll probably want to come here."

Both police officers helped the census worker pick up her questionnaires. McGill said, "Go with Dixon to a squad car. Give her a complete statement, and then call your boss." He looked up to see the detective with the crime scene team. "Stay here. Tell your boss not to come until you give him the clear, okay?"

Laura Beth nodded. She went with the officer to wait. Dixon gave her paper and pen to write out her statement. Then, Laura Beth called her supervisor and told him what had happened and that she'd file the proper paperwork. Thinking about her work kept her calm. Finished talking to Blanchard, she called her husband and took a deep breath, knowing Bruce would probably throw a fit.

After calming her near-crazed husband and assuring him she was safe, she sat on the seat inside the cruiser with the door open. She thumbed through her EQs and found the proper form to fill out for an incident. Finding a pencil in her fanny pack, she began the process of reporting anything unusual and the fact that someone besides herself had touched the confidential questionnaires.

Dixon squinted at her charge. "I gave you a pen."

"I know, but all forms have to be done in number two pencil. Computers."

"Ah. Will you be okay if I join my boss?"

"Sure."

~

Before the crime scene team finished, three more black SUVs roared into the complex. Half a dozen people, five men and a woman, exited the vehicles, all wearing the pigeon-holed black suits—*FBI,* Laura Beth surmised. *Why?*

The apparent leader of the team cornered Detective McGill very near where Laura Beth sat. She strained to hear what was being said. The man in the black suit explained to the local cop, "Her name was actually Consuela Garcia-Perez. This was to be her relocation for witness protection."

"Shoddy job."

"You have no idea." He lowered his voice. "Second dead witness."

"Real shoddy job. I thought U.S. Marshalls and WITSEC had a reputation for never losing a person."

"Apparently that reputation just got shot to hell." The FBI agent grunted. "I need to talk to your witness."

McGill nodded toward the cruiser. "Mrs. Copeland is waiting there. I need to get back to investigating. Are you planning to take over?"

"Let's cooperate."

A snort preceded, "Yeah, right." McGill left the other man to do what needed to be done.

The census worker sat up straight as the squat, barrel-chested man with red splotches on his face came toward her. In a sandpaper voice, the fireplug in a black suit said, "Mrs. Copeland, correct?"

"Yes."

"I need you to tell me everything you saw, heard, smelled, touched or tasted. No detail is too small."

"May I see your identification?"

The heavy-set agent chuckled. "Sure." He pulled out his credentials and a small recorder. "You should be wary, Mrs. Copeland."

Still shaken, the woman nodded as the agent returned the badge to his inside coat pocket. "I heard you say something about witness protection. Why is the FBI involved and so quickly? You *are* FBI according to that badge, Agent Pickering."

"Yes and no. OCB."

"OCB?"

"Organized Crime Bureau."

"She's Mafia?" came out in a high-pitched squeak.

The man sat on the grassy curb in front of the only witness to anything. "No. There's a great deal more to organized crime than the Mafia. The Racketeer Influenced and Corrupt Organizations Act encompasses a lot. We deal with gangs, organized prostitution, drug distribution, and anything else that might fall under the RICO statutes. Maria Biaggi was in witness protection. She testified in a high-profile case against a Mexican drug lord. Her real name was Consuela Garcia-Perez."

Her hand flying to her mouth, Laura Beth mumbled, "I saw that on the news. She testified against her own husband in Houston."

"Yes, and we thought we had hidden her well. U.S. Marshalls were completing the relocation process." He pointed toward the other agents. "Two of them. They *ain't* happy."

"I can understand why. Agent Pickering, how can I help? I really did *not* see anything."

"Any detail would help." He held up the recorder. "Mind?"

She shook her head. Laura Beth gave her vital statistics at the man's request and told the agent about her first encounter with the dead woman and why she had come back to try again. "I saw"—She fanned her face with her hands—"The head through the cracks in the blinds. Then, the Escalade zoomed by."

"Are you sure it was an Escalade?"

"Yes, I saw the Cadillac symbol. Why?"

He pointed toward the black SUVs the federal agents had arrived in. All were Escalades.

"Oh," she whispered. "No, Agent Pickering, I saw the Cadillac symbol."

"But not the driver?"

She shook her head. "It was a man. I saw a silhouette through the dark glass."

"Thin? Fat?"

Laura Beth knitted her brows together. "He seemed to have a very large nose."

"How could you tell?"

"I'm a photographer by trade, at least that's my degree—photography. I notice these things."

"Anything else?"

"No. I'm sorry. Wait. I think he had a blue tooth device. I saw blinking near where his ear should have been."

Agent Pickering turned off the recorder, stood, and dusted fresh-mowed grass from his trousers. Laura Beth smiled slightly. "Aren't you burning up in that suit? It gets hot in Mississippi early. It's only late April and I've already had to run the air conditioner."

Pickering ran a stubby index finger under the collar of his starched white shirt. "I'm suffocating, Mrs. Copeland, but I have a job to do."

"Where's her body?"

The agent looked down into alert chocolate-colored eyes. "My bet would be in the back of that Escalade."

"Agent Pickering, how did they find her if she was in witness protection?"

He ran a pudgy hand through thinning mousy brown hair. *An inside job.* "I don't know," he said aloud. "McGill says you have to file some kind of report because you dropped your questionnaires and your boss might come." He looked toward the gate where a black Mercedes waited. "Does he drive a Mercedes?"

In the gathering twilight, Laura Beth stood and followed the agent's gaze. "No. That's my husband."

"He's concerned. I take it the Jag is yours?"

"Yes."

"Why are you doing the census? Looks like you have money."

"I thought it would be interesting."

A low chuckle gave way to, "Looks like you got your wish. Bet you don't find a head every day." He handed her a card. "This gives new meaning to counting heads, I'd say. Call me if you think of anything else, or if you need anything. Go take care of your business now."

~

Dr. Bruce Copeland fawned over his pregnant wife. "You sure you're not hurt?"

"No, Bruce. I just got the wits scared out of me."

As they spoke, Laura Beth's supervisor, Doug Blanchard, arrived. He sounded as worried as Bruce. "Mrs. Copeland, are you all right?"

Laura Beth held up a stiff hand. "I'm not the one without a head." She explained to both men what had occurred and sorted through the EQs that had spilled to the concrete. "Sorry about having to file an incident report, Mr. Blanchard."

"Not your fault, honey."

She handed him the form already complete. "I didn't have anything else to do while I waited for the police to talk to me," she said to the surprised expression on the older man's face. She looked around as Detective Sergeant McGill approached them.

"Sergeant?"

"Mrs. Copeland, there's nothing else you can do here tonight. Might I suggest you work a different area for a few days, and"— He pointed toward Pickering—"one of us might need to speak with you again."

"Of course, I'll send her elsewhere," snorted Blanchard.

"Maybe you shouldn't do this at all," Bruce said.

Laura Beth coughed lightly before she introduced the two men to the police officer. The tall, muscular detective shook hands with both men and smiled at Bruce. "Dr. Copeland, Bruce, it's been a

while."

"Yes, it has, Tanner. What three years?"

The blond cop nodded. Laura Beth looked back and forth between the two men. "Did I miss something?"

"No," replied her husband with a shake of his dark-brown wavy hair.

McGill explained, "Bruce was my wife's doctor. She had breast cancer."

"Oh!" Laura Beth touched her fingers to her lips. "Is she?"

"I'm afraid so," said McGill. "She left me an eleven-year-old and an eight-year old, now—seven and four at the time. A boy and a girl, Corbin and Roslyn."

"I'm so sorry. You're the second person I've met in the past week who's had professional dealings with my husband."

"Dr. Copeland did everything he could do. Now, you need to go home and try to relax after this ordeal. Expect a call in a day or two." The policeman nodded and went back to work.

Bruce caressed his wife's arm. "Are you okay to drive home?"

She nodded. "Follow me."

~

Laura Beth tried to sleep, but she was awakened twice dreaming the head she saw was screaming at her. The black Escalade squealed by her and tried to hit her, causing her to jolt awake. She switched on the bedside lamp and snatched a notepad and pen from the drawer in the nightstand, hastily sketching the outline of the face she saw in her dream. She was certain it was the same profile she had seen that evening.

Bruce sat up beside her. "Are you okay?"

She rubbed her face as if trying to restore feeling to her cheeks. "Yeah. Just a bad dream, but I remembered a little more about the driver of the SUV. I drew what I saw." She handed the sketch to her husband.

"Not much to go on, baby."

"I know, but Agent Pickering said any little thing."

"Other than looking like Jimmy Durante's nose and Earnest Borgnine's chin, you don't have much here." He chuckled softly. "If this guy actually looks like this from the side, I bet he's one ugly cuss."

She slapped her husband on the arm. "You're awful."

Bruce laughed and laid the pad on his nightstand. He reached for Laura Beth's face and kissed her. "Feel up to trying to think about something else?"

"Does the doctor have a prescription?"

"Oh, yeah." He rolled on top of her and scooted beneath the covers until just his head showed. "Any way you want to do it, baby."

"I just love being in control."

3
Eight Heads in a Duffle Bag

After Dr. Copeland left for work at seven the next morning, Laura Beth called Agent Pickering who asked her to bring in what she had. She told him she'd be at his temporary office in the police station as soon as she dropped her two children at her church's "Mother's Morning Out" program.

As the agent waited for his only hope of identifying a killer to arrive, he reviewed Laura Beth's statement. *Big nose? I'm ninety-nine percent certain we have a traitor among us. But who? I don't have anyone with an unusually large nose.* For a second, he felt his own and laughed. *Except me. Unless...Naa.* He shook his head hard at the thought. *I've known him for years.*

A knock at his open door drew his attention away from his dilemma for a moment. The agent waved in Detective Sergeant McGill and pointed to a chair. McGill sat. "Any news? You promised to keep me in the loop."

"Mrs. Copeland had a dream and drew the face she thinks she saw. She's bringing her *mug* shot in."

"Well, it's something. So, Perez is dead and so is Montegna in some little Podunk town in Louisiana?"

"Eau Boueuse—about the same size as Sunrise. Yeah. That Detective Reynolds down there lambasted the Feds. I guess we deserve it."

"You know"—McGill placed his hands on his knees and sat forward—"If you did keep the locals informed, we could be more help than you think."

"Not my call, but you might be right. Hey, I wouldn't even have been brought in on this if Montegna hadn't ended up only a head."

"What about the other three who testified? I'm assuming they're spread out all over the country." He leaned back.

"I've sent agents to check on them, but I haven't heard anything yet. It was like pulling teeth to get the Marshall Service to tell me where to find them." Pickering rubbed his ruddy forehead. "I'm getting a headache thinking about it."

"I have the cure for that." McGill left and returned with a steaming cup of liquid that did not smell like coffee.

"What is it? Poison?" Pickering grinned wryly.

"Sassafras tea. It's good for what ails you."

The federal agent took the mug and sipped the concoction. "Tastes like root beer without the fizz."

McGill sat back down. "My grandmother used to swear by it. It can't hurt you. That's for sure."

"Tastes okay. If it doesn't kill me, I'll thank your grandma."

"You'll have to light a candle to do it, but thanks for the thought."

Agent Pickering's cell buzzed. He answered and his face blanched as he listened. "What?" McGill demanded when the other man hung up.

"Number three head in East Lyme, Connecticut. Carlos said heads would roll. He apparently meant literally."

"Whoa! I'd hate to be you."

"I'm hating being me, but let's not forget they weren't in my charge." He finished the tea. "The only clue we have besides Mrs. Copeland is that apparently Montegna, and it looks like Perez, were killed with one swift cut of a very sharp blade, maybe something like a Samurai sword. Our killer might have serious martial arts training. "

"Did you send the remains to the Crime Lab in Jackson?"

"Yeah. The medical examiner rushed the results, but knowing *how* Perez was killed, doesn't help a whole lot. I have nothing at the scene to point me in the direction of a person."

Another knock at the door caught both men off guard. "Dixon, what's up?" asked McGill.

"Boss, this was just delivered to the front desk. It's addressed to Agent Pickering and there's a card." The female officer held up a UPS box.

The agent scowled. "Did you think to put on gloves?"

The woman looked at her hands. "Um. Oops. Sorry."

"Who delivered it?" asked McGill.

"Kincaid," Dixon replied.

Pickering looked at McGill. McGill said, "Local UPS guy." McGill waved his hand toward the floor. "Set it down." He looked at the agent. "A bomb? Anthrax? Do we need the dogs?"

"I doubt it. If it were poisoned, we might already have a dead cop." He glowered at Dixon. "Let's see what I got." The agent slipped on latex gloves and held his hand out for the card. He carefully opened the envelope and read the cryptic typed message:

> *Happy birthday. Merry Christmas. Don't you smell a rat?*

"Well, well." He knelt beside the box and with precision opened it. Inside was a non-descript army-green canvas duffle bag. Before he did anything else, he called one of his forensics agents. Then, he hesitantly unzipped it. "Shit!" He sat with a thud onto the floor. "McGill, I think I got my answer."

The local detective peered over the agent's shoulder. Inside the duffle bag were eight-by-ten photos of the severed heads of the five witnesses, a close-up shot of the agent's head, and a close-up picture of Laura Beth Copeland's head. All were framed in black metal certificate frames.

"Oh, hell," McGill moaned. "You and your witness have just been threatened."

"Yep, I think so—or is it a warning? If our killer thinks she can identify him, Mrs. Copeland is not safe."

~

Laura Beth dropped her two children at the church and was assured three full hours of time to do whatever she pleased. She glanced at the hastily drawn sketch on the seat beside her. *Maybe I'm being foolish. It was a dream, not real.* Nonetheless, she turned down the shady, narrow back street where ancient oaks spread a canopy, causing sunlight to flicker on the windshield. *This little town isn't used to this kind of drama. It's always been so safe.* She sighed.

Driving carefully through the neighborhood of older houses owned by older people, Laura Beth checked her speedometer and her rearview mirror as a matter of habit. Her heartrate increased when she saw a black Escalade a discreet distance behind her.

She fumbled in her purse for the card Pickering had given her and clumsily dialed the number with one hand. The agent answered, still sitting beside the duffle bag. "Pickering."

"Agent Pickering, this is Laura Beth Copeland. I'm on my way, but there's a black Escalade behind me."

"Following you?"

"I don't know."

"Where exactly are you?"

"I'm traveling down Shady Oak Drive to get to Main Street."

Laura Beth could hear the agent talking to someone. "Get a squad car out to Shady Oak Drive." The agent came back to her. "Take your next right and see if it turns after you. Stay on the phone. What street will it be?"

She glanced at the street sign. "Maple."

"Shady Oak and Maple," the agent said to whoever was in the room with him.

Laura Beth took the turn. The SUV drove past. "It passed the intersection and didn't turn after me."

"Good. It might just be a coincidence but come on here right now. We've already stopped three black SUV's since yesterday evening, even if they weren't Escalades. Still, don't take a chance."

Laura Beth saw flashing blue lights when she turned back onto Shady Oak and a stocky, bald, black man standing beside the Escalade. *Coincidence. Just a coincidence.* She breathed a sigh of relief.

Laura Beth turned onto Main Street. A black Escalade pulled from a parking space and headed the other direction.

~

Laura Beth entered the police station, her sketch clasped tightly in her hand. She was escorted to Agent Pickering who had placed the duffle bag on his desk to await a forensics team. McGill waited with the agent.

Both men stood when Laura Beth entered the room. She smiled at them, feeling safe in their presence. "Agent Pickering. Detective McGill." She thrust the drawing toward the agent.

"Please sit down, Mrs. Copeland," Pickering said.

Laura Beth sat in the chair beside McGill. "Hmmm," grunted Pickering and shared the sketch that resembled a caricature with McGill.

"That's one butt-ugly mug," McGill said.

Laura Beth chuckled softly. "That's what Bruce said."

"Are you sure this isn't just dream-induced?"

She shrugged. "No. But it seems right."

Pickering nodded. "I appreciate you even trying. By the way, the driver of that Escalade is an attorney. Could you tell if the driver of the suspect car was black or white?"

"No. I just got a shape of a profile. That's what I drew." She scrunched her eyes. "I *think* the hair might have been pulled into a ponytail though." She eyed the duffle bag in a large evidence box. "Traveling soon?"

"No. This is evidence that I'm waiting to have examined."

McGill started to speak. Pickering shook his head. Laura Beth caught the exchange. "Should I know something?"

"Stay alert," Pickering encouraged. "What you did today was the right thing. This person might think you can identify him."

McGill spoke up, "Mrs. Copeland, I think it would be best if you hold off on your census-taking for a little while."

"Am I in some kind of danger?"

The men exchanged a knowing look. McGill said, "I think you should show her."

Pickering huffed and unzipped the duffle bag. "Take a look."

Hand over her mouth, Laura Beth stifled a squeaky scream. "That's *my* picture. Where did you get that? It was taken last night while we were in front of Maria Biaggi's apartment. Those are the earrings I wore last night."

"Yeah." Pickering pointed to his own photo. "Mine too. See the reflection of the patrol car lights?"

A knock at the door startled the trio. A member of the forensics team entered the office. "Ah, just who I needed to see," said Pickering, adding Laura Beth's sketch to the evidence box containing the duffle bag.

"See if you can get anything from the bag, the note, the pics, and the frames. Then, see if anyone can use this sketch and get a face." Pickering handed the evidence to the man from the Crime Lab in the state capital. "This is nowhere nearly as funny as the movie, but here are your *Eight Heads in a Duffle Bag*. The next one to roll is the drawing. I swear it."

4
Fender Bender

Before Laura Beth left Agent Pickering's makeshift office, agents from around the country had verified the five witnesses against Carlos Perez were dead, decapitated and the bodies still missing. Pickering growled, "The son of a bitch still won't get out of jail. This was simple revenge."

The agent looked at the lady who had been thrust into a dangerous situation. "Call me when you get home. I want to know you're safe."

"I appreciate your concern. I've got to pick my kids up and then it's off to home."

McGill muttered, "There's a long stretch of road out Highway 278 toward your house that's rather isolated. Keep both eyes open."

"I will."

Laura Beth left, and the two law enforcement officers continued to discuss the case and the woman. McGill groaned, "We don't have enough to get a watch on her."

"I know. She's a cute little thing, isn't she? But I bet she has a temper."

"A cute little mother of two with another one on the way. If this jerk hurts her and causes that baby to die, that's manslaughter in Mississippi. But I guess that would just be another notch on his belt."

"Any chance of an unofficial watch?"

"I have limited manpower. Cops like to get paid, you know."

"And such a salary it is." Pickering stood. "It's your turn to buy lunch."

"We've never had lunch. Why is it *my* turn?"

"I'm company." Pickering gave the local a toothy grin.

"Fine." McGill slapped his legs and stood. "I'm taking you to the greasiest place I know, but also the best food in town—Gus's Goulash."

~

Laura Beth picked up her two daughters, and the girls began to chant, "McDonald's," with little fists striking their legs in a drum-like rhythm.

The mother laughed. "Did you two little imps plan this?"

"Please, Mommy?" begged Stacey.

Tonya echoed, "Pwease?"

A sigh showed Laura Beth's resignation. "Well, we do have to eat, but we're going through the drive-thru and going home. No playland today." Auburn waves fell over her shoulders as she shook her head for emphasis.

"Awww," the girls whined.

"No. Mommy needs to go home."

Laura Beth stuck to her decision and ordered two chicken nugget kids' meals with fruit and milk. She ordered herself a chicken sandwich meal with fruit and milk. She rubbed her slightly protruding abdomen. "We all have to eat healthy food, but I sure would like some fries."

When the attendant handed the bags through the window, Laura Beth placed them on the passenger's seat. Instant kicking to the back of her seat brought a scolding and Stacey demanded, "Can't we eat in the car? I'm hungry."

"Stop kicking the seat. We'll be home in fifteen minutes."

"Mommy?"

Brown eyes peered into her rearview mirror. "No, young lady," she said firmly. "You will live until we get home. After lunch both of you are taking a nap."

The little girl snorted and folded her arms. Laura Beth could not help but chuckle as the child looked so much like her having a tantrum. Her sister looked more like Bruce with her dark hair and hazel eyes constantly changing color with each outfit she wore.

Laura Beth turned onto Highway 278 to go home. Driving a mile or two over the speed limit, she checked her rearview mirror frequently. *Nobody back there.* She heaved a great sigh as the two girls began to bicker.

"Girls! Stop unless you want no TV tonight at all."

Stacey stuck her tongue out at her sister. "I saw that," said Laura Beth.

"How?" asked the little girl.

"Mommies have eyes in the backs of their heads."

"Nuh, huh."

The mother glanced over her shoulder. "You are pushing your luck."

The long stretch McGill had mentioned was coming up. Laura Beth checked her mirror again. No one was behind her, but a log truck was approaching from the other direction. Logging was a main profession in the area, so she felt no concern about the truck. Suddenly, from behind the semi, a dark SUV pulled around as if intending to pass.

Laura Beth watched briefly, but the car seemed to be matching the truck's speed rather than accelerating to pass. The vehicle was in such a position that the truck driver would be unaware of its presence. She squinted into the sunlight. *This can't be real. That's a black Escalade.*

The wary mother slowed. *Come on. Pass already.*

Laura Beth reached for her purse to get her cell phone, but it tumbled to the floor. She bit her tongue not to say a bad word the girls would repeat. She slowed more.

The Escalade showed no sign of altering its path. It was headed directly toward Laura Beth's forest-green Jaguar. Laura Beth inched toward the shoulder. The emergency parking lane was narrow on the back highway.

At the last second, the Cadillac whipped in front of the truck and zoomed away. The trucker laid on his horn. Laura Beth jerked her car toward the shoulder and fishtailed in the loose gravel on the side of the road. The car bumped down the low incline and into a small pine. Laura Beth's airbag deployed. "Shit!" escaped her lips before she could control her tongue.

"Mommy, you cussed," Stacey whimpered.

Stacey and Tonya began to wail in the backseat. The next sound Laura Beth heard was banging on her window. A tall, thin black man stood there.

In shock, the woman lowered her window a fraction. "Are you okay?" asked the man. "That jerk ran you off the road. Sorry I didn't see him in my mirror. He was in my blind spot."

Laura Beth glanced in her side mirror. She realized the trucker had stopped and come to help her. "Call the police," she said. "Ask for Detective McGill or Agent Pickering."

The trucker looked down the road. "Yeah, you're still in city limits. Barely." The man pulled out a cell phone and made the call. Then he helped Laura Beth from the car after pushing the deflated airbag out of the way.

"Girls, stop!" Laura Beth scolded as the children bellowed.

The man addressed the two girls. "You little ladies wanna go sit in the big truck? I got some cookies in the sleeper.

"You're a little upset and it's hard to think right now." He grinned at the woman. "I got three. Is it okay if I give 'em a cookie? They can take a nap in the sleeper. It might take a little time for the cops to sort this mess out."

"Sure. Thanks." She rubbed her forearms as bruises already had begun to form. "I'm too short for that air bag."

The trucker got the girls out and led them to his rig. He situated them in the small sleeping compartment and gave them cookies and juice pouches he had in a cooler.

Stacey said, "We got chicken nuggets in the car if they didn't spill on the floor."

"I'll check on that for you, but for now sit in there."

A couple of cars passed without stopping although the drivers slowed to view the accident scene. The man came back to the car. "They want their chicken nuggets."

"I was too abrupt with them." Laura Beth rubbed her head and laughed. "They don't realize what just happened. Did you by any chance get the license plate?"

"No ma'am. I sorta was looking to see if you were okay."

"Thanks for stopping."

The man walked to the passenger's side and looked on the seat. "Mind if I take the girls their food?"

"Not at all. Thanks. You're a nice man."

As the trucker took the Happy Meals to the children, McGill, Pickering and a highway patrol officer roared onto the scene. Despite the situation, Laura Beth almost laughed at the stain on Pickering's shirt where his lunch had dripped. Though his appearance was a bit madcap, she felt he could be a reckoning force.

"Are you all right?" were the first words out of the agent's mouth.

Tanner took her hands. "She's bruised."

"The air bags," she said. "I'm not injured."

Laura Beth told them what happened. The truck driver confirmed the part about the Escalade whipping in front of him and forcing the Jaguar off the road. He was unaware the driver of the SUV had been beside him for some time.

A tow truck arrived and pulled the car back onto the road. The bumper was bent, and the airbags needed to be repacked, but nobody was seriously injured, and the damage was minimal.

McGill said, "You'll have to take it into a garage to repack the bags. I bet you have to go to the dealer to get most of the work done."

"Detective, this was deliberate," Laura Beth mumbled.

"Looks that way. Looks like a warning to be quiet."

"What can I say?" She splayed both hands in the air, palms toward the sky. "I've told the authorities all I know."

"But he thinks you can identify him."

"Do you think he'll try something else?"

Pickering came over after talking with the truck driver. "He might. You want one of us to give you a ride home? Where are you sending the car?"

The tow truck driver said, "It'll have to go to the dealership to get those bags repacked according to standard."

Laura Beth sighed. "Jackson Jaguar."

The man handed her the chicken sandwich and her purse. "Anything else you need, ma'am?"

"Yeah. The booster seats."

"Most insurance companies offer rentals with your policy," the tow truck driver said. "And road-side assistance."

"I'll do it tomorrow." She looked at McGill. "Can you take us home?"

"Sure. Your girls are having an adventure today. First a big rig, now a police car. Should I run the lights and siren?"

Laura Beth laughed even in the face of danger. "Only a father would ask that. I bet they'll love it."

~

Tanner ran the lights and the siren all the way to Laura Beth's house. The girls thought it was cool and jabbered on the short trip.

The spacious, one-story ranch-style house was situated just outside the city limits on twenty acres of land, partly left wooded for effect. The immediate area near the house was meticulously, professionally landscaped with boxwoods along the wrap-around veranda and flowerbeds bordered by railroad ties strategically and symmetrically placed in the yard. Two Bradford pear trees heralded the beginning of the packed gravel driveway.

Before he let Laura Beth and the girls out of the car, Tanner did a quick walk around the house but saw nothing significantly out of place. The back window was cracked, but it was not unusual for people in the country to open windows in lieu of running the air conditioner.

Laura Beth opened the door and turned off the alarm. Tanner dipped the corners of his mouth. *As I suspected. Just ventilation. Nothing else seems off at all.*

Not ten minutes after she entered the house, the phone rang. Laura Beth answered. Tanner listened and gathered the call was friendly. He could hear Laura Beth telling someone what had happened. She ended with, "We're fine, Penny, but I'll let you know if I need you."

She's friends with the sheriff, the detective thought. *Good, because she's in the county.*

McGill stayed at the Copeland house until Bruce got home. The doctor was in a tizzy. "Damn it, Laura Beth! Somebody tried to kill you."

"Sh." She waved her hands. "Don't scare the girls. I was already mean to them when this happened."

Bruce clutched his wife's hands. "And you look like you've been in the boxing ring."

"The air bags did that, Bruce. Calm down."

Hoping to prevent what was fast becoming an argument, McGill intervened. "I think it was a warning. If he had meant to kill her, she'd be dead." The detective looked somber. "This is a professional hitman, but I think somebody on the inside is on the take."

"You mean a cop?" asked Bruce, placing a protective arm around Laura Beth's shoulders.

"Not a local because we didn't even know we had a witness to protect."

"Pickering?"

"Naa." Tanner's blond hair revealed even blonder highlights as the light reflected when he shook his head. "He's a good man and trying to put the pieces together."

"What can *you* do?"

"If anything else happens, I'll get surveillance on Mrs. Copeland and the house."

Bruce demanded, "Why not now?"

"Budget and the house *is* in the county. I'd have to coordinate with the sheriff."

The doctor looked as if he would explode. Laura Beth laid her hand on his chest. "Honey, Tanner's doing all he can."

The detective's dimples showed slightly at the familiarity. "Yes, I am, Bruce. I'll do everything in my power to protect Laura Beth."

Bruce nodded. "I understand you can't do anything, but Sheriff Ulmer lives next door."

Tanner laughed. "Out here next door is a good way off. I'll talk to her if necessary." He cut Laura Beth a look.

"I talked to Penny today," she informed her husband. "She said to let her know if anything happens out here."

"Let me get back now that you're home, Bruce," Tanner said. "Lock up and stay vigilant. Don't hesitate to call."

The detective left and Bruce pulled his wife into his arms. The next order of business was getting the car taken care of.

5
Rat's in the Cradle

Bruce spent over an hour on the phone taking care of his wife's car situation. The dealership told him the car would be ready by the end of the week. He then made arrangements for a rental car to be delivered to the house.

While he took care of the insurance company and the others involved in repairing Laura Beth's car, she prepared dinner. When Bruce came into the kitchen, he watched his two daughters as they helped their mother. Both girls sat on the kitchen island. Stacey buttered sliced French bread to make garlic bread while Tonya tore lettuce into chunks to begin salad. Laura Beth stirred spaghetti sauce at the stove.

Bruce smiled at the scene. He took a deep breath, inhaling the comfort of the kitchen aromas of tomato, garlic and oregano. He walked in and kissed the girls on the cheek and his wife at the nape of her neck. "It smells delicious."

"Are all the arrangements made?" asked Laura Beth.

"Yes. Your car will be fixed by Friday, and Enterprise will deliver a Camry for you to use tomorrow morning. It'll have to be returned when you go to pick up your car."

"What time in the morning?"

"Around ten."

"It's a good thing I don't have any plans."

"You can finish the nursery."

"Good idea." She drained the pasta and asked, "Will you put the bread in the oven for seven minutes? Sprinkle garlic salt first."

"Sure."

Laura Beth lifted the girls down and told them to set the table. She then added grated carrots, thinly sliced cucumber, tiny pieces of broccoli, cherry tomatoes, grated cheese, chopped eggs, and bacon bits to the salad and tossed it. When the oven dinged indicating the bread was done, the family sat down to dinner.

~

Bruce left his home at seven to begin chemotherapy for patients scheduled for that day. His clinic was an extension of University Medical Center where he would send patients too advanced for his help. He kissed his wife and left her with a warning. "Make the Enterprise person show you some I.D. before you let anyone in; and if it's not a white Camry, don't take it. That's the one they said they'd deliver."

"Yes, darling."

"I love you. I'd be lost without you."

"I'll be careful, Bruce. I'm going to stencil the different sports balls on the nursery wall. If anything weird happens, I'll call Tanner and you. It's nice to have a friend on the force."

Bruce sighed. "I wish I could've done more for his wife. By the time she came in after ignoring symptoms, all I could do was manage her pain and watch her die. It was too late even for the hospital."

Laura Beth caressed her husband's cheek. "Tanner said you did your best. I know you did." She kissed his lips softly.

"Mmm. Wish I could stay home after that kiss."

"Come home early."

He bumped his forehead to hers and went to take care of his patients.

~

Laura Beth peeked into the large airy room in sunshine yellow, white trim, and a border of daisies where her two little girls still slept in white canopy beds. Though there were several more rooms, the girls wanted to share a room at this age. *They'll change their minds as teens.* She closed the door softly to keep from waking them. She went into the laundry room where she retrieved the wall stencils and a basket of small paint cans in several colors. The thought of watching her husband pound homeruns and shoot amazing golf scores for their college teams brought a smile to her face. She caressed the golf bag that sat in the corner and looked up at her tennis racquet that had been idle for a long time. She rubbed her stomach as the baby moved. "Once you get here, I'm hitting the tennis court again." Picking up the painting supplies, she headed to the room across the hall from where the girls slept.

Bruce and she had already painted the walls of the nursery sky blue. Stenciling the sports items was her husband's idea, but she had agreed. He had moved in the handcrafted light oak cradle her father-in-law had made for the first child, along with the matching changing table and chest of drawers. Laura Beth smiled again remembering how excited Bruce's dad had been when they walked around the flea market and she had told him she wanted a cradle when she got pregnant. The day she called to tell him his first grandchild was on the way, the man had bought the wood and made the set. His woodworking hobby had become a second income and now a retirement income over the years.

Balancing the supplies on one arm and her hip, she turned the doorknob and pushed the door open with her other hip. She held the door open with her toe while she set the paint on the floor and then quietly closed the door. She picked up the supplies and headed across the room to where the cradle rested near the bay window so she could raise the window to ventilate the paint fumes. The window was already open and the screen off.

Laura Beth dropped everything and let out a blood-curdling scream before she fumed, "Oh, hell no! The bastard was coming from my house yesterday. How did he get in without the alarm going off?"

Two little girls ran into the room with their mother, their silky night gowns fluttering in the breeze. "Out!" Laura Beth commanded.

"What's wrong, Mommy?" asked Stacey.

"Go to the kitchen. I'll be there in a second." The girls hesitated. "Go!" Laura Beth pointed sharply, and the children obeyed.

The angry redhead marched to her bedroom, picked up the house phone and called Detective McGill. "You have to see this," she said when he answered. "I need to call Bruce, but he has chemo patients today. They need him."

"What's happened?"

"He broke into the house yesterday. When he ran me off the road, he was coming from my house. The car accident was not intended, but he took advantage of the situation. He recognized my car, but he had been in my house."

"How do you know?"

"The window in the nursery."

"You didn't leave that open?"

"No."

"But you had to turn off the alarm when we went in."

"I'm not the cop here!" she screeched.

"Okay. Calm. You're out of the city limits. I have no jurisdiction, but I'll come and bring Pickering. Call the sheriff. I'll see you in a few."

~

Once again, Laura Beth was surrounded by law enforcement. Agent Pickering stared into the cradle at a gutted, dead rat and blood smeared over the mattress. He sang, "'Rat's in the cradle and silver spoon; Little Boy Blue and the Man in the Moon.'"

"Are you nuts?" snapped Laura Beth, popping her hands onto her hips, arms akimbo. "First of all, it's, 'Cat's in the cradle.' Second, the lunatic was in my house, and that looks like a threat to my children." She stomped to the top drawer of the bureau in the master bedroom and returned with a .357 magnum. "I will blow his brains all over the wall."

"Is that loaded?" asked McGill.

"Of course, it's loaded. What good is an unloaded gun? I keep it locked up, but it's loaded."

Hands pushing gently on the air, McGill said, "Put it back. You don't need it right now."

Chin jutted in defiance, she returned the gun to its safe place. McGill muttered, "That damned gun's bigger than she is."

"But I shoot straight, Tanner," Laura Beth said when she walked back in.

The sheriff ushered everyone from the room as her own forensics team came to dust for prints and process the scene. Sheriff Penny Ulmer stated, "Pickering and McGill have brought me up to date since last night. Why didn't you call me first this morning?"

"I um…"

"It doesn't matter." Ulmer waved a hand. "I think the rat was a warning. He really thinks you can identify him. Can you, Laura Beth?"

"No better than I already have."

"Well, you don't have neighbors to have seen anything. Let's hope the team turns up something."

Laura Beth took a deep breath. "I guess y'all would like some coffee?"

"Thanks a million." Ulmer grinned, her front teeth slightly gapped, but her green eyes sparkling against her caramel complexion.

Laura Beth set about making coffee and feeding her daughters Fruit Loops for breakfast. After a good length of time one of the investigators came into the kitchen. "Sheriff, we got a cast of a boot print. Looks to be about a size eleven."

"What kind of boot?"

"Cowboy. I think our guy could be from Texas where the Perez case was tried."

Pickering sniggered. "Well, gang. Now we have a cowboy with a big nose and bulldog chin."

Laura Beth cut him a look. He sobered. "Anything else?"

"No, sir. No prints besides the family."

"How about the rat?"

"What about it?"

"How was it killed?"

"From the way it was gutted, I'd say hunting knife."

"So? A cowboy hunter with a big nose and bulldog chin." Pickering winked at Laura Beth. "Sheriff, it might be time for some police protection."

"Don't know if I can get approval with just a dead rat."

"Oh, for Pete's sake, Penny!" exclaimed Laura Beth. "You're my friend and next-door neighbor."

"But the taxpayers pay for anything I do." She lifted her hands in the air. "Hey, I can lend you Leather and Lace though their bark might be worse than their bite. They'd probably lick him to death. At least they're big and would scare the sh..., um, mess out of the guy."

Laura Beth ground her teeth. "He'd probably take off their heads too."

The clanging of her house phone made everyone in the room jump in fright. She grabbed the receiver from the kitchen counter to hear her husband demanding to know what was going on. She told him as calmly as she could and hung up. Her hand had barely laid the phone back in its cradle when it blared again. She snatched it up. "Bruce, the cops are taking care of it."

A whisper said, "Apparently, you didn't get the message. Too bad. I was hoping to spare someone as pretty as you."

6
Prepaid Cell Phone

Eyes wide with fear, Laura Beth held the receiver out toward Pickering. He cocked his eyebrow in question. "It's him," she mouthed.

Pickering seized the receiver. "This is Agent Pickering."

A low chuckle met his ear. "Gutsy little broad."

The agent gave frantic hand signals to McGill to get someone to start a triangulation on the call. McGill used his cell phone to call the phone company.

Pickering said into the mouthpiece, "Leave Mrs. Copeland alone. She doesn't know anything. All she could tell us is that a black Escalade left the parking lot about the time she found Mrs. Perez's remains."

"Yeah, right. That's why she came in to see you again."

"How did Perez manage to hire you?"

The man on the other end of the phone laughed. "You think you can keep me talking long enough to find me. I'm not an amateur. If I were stationary, I'd be off in about half a minute more. As it is, I'm moving and, dumbass, this is a prepaid phone. You can't track me."

"Listen, you don't have to stalk this woman. I'm telling you she knows nothing."

"Yeah. Sure thing." A long sigh came over the wire. "You've forced a hand. I've really tried here. I have to do some things I'd rather not. For the record—*Perez* didn't hire me."

The line went dead. "Damn it!" hollered Pickering.

McGill came back into the kitchen. "He hung up?"

"Yeah. Anything? I know you didn't have much time."

McGill rolled his eyes. "Once I got through to a human being, the techno geeks at the phone company confirmed the location within a five-mile radius, but no way to trace the call to a person."

"Prepaid. He told me."

Laura Beth looked stricken. "He's close to us right now?"

McGill nodded and stepped away to make another phone call.

The phone rang again. Laura Beth nearly jumped out of her skin. Pickering signaled again and nodded for her to pick up. "Hello," she said into the receiver.

"Why didn't you break off whatever call you were on?" Bruce Copeland demanded.

Laura Beth shook her head. "It's Bruce."

"Oh," Pickering said. "Your call waiting beeped while I was talking to the nut."

"What's going on?" asked Bruce.

After a deep sigh, his wife replied, "He called me. Bruce, now I *am* actually scared." She looked up with big brown eyes at all the law enforcement around her. "He's been in our house, which means he somehow bypassed our security system. I feel violated, and he threatened my children. He's already run us off the road."

McGill came in. "I have police and Penny has deputies sweeping the area for a black Escalade. You said he was mobile, right, Pickering?"

"Is Tanner there?" asked Bruce.

"Yes, along with Agent Pickering and Penny Ulmer and a dozen other cops," answered Laura Beth.

"Then, you're safe for the time being. I'll be home as soon as I can. If everyone else leaves, see if either Pickering or Tanner can stay until I get there. I have three more patients."

"Kay." Her voice quivered.

"I love you, baby. Keep somebody there."

"Love you more."

A light chuckle helped to calm Laura Beth. Bruce finished their little routine. "I love you most."

~

As the county crime scene team finished their investigation of the premises, three more federal agents arrived. Pickering groaned.

"What's wrong?" asked McGill.

"My boss sent reinforcements."

"That's a good thing," said Laura Beth. "It gives you more people."

"Two of them are okay, but I can't stand Montoya."

"Which one is he?"

"The one with the prominent…"

Pickering looked at Laura Beth. "Naa. He's been in Texas undercover for over two years. He's an asshole, but—"

Laura Beth made a face at the man and cut her eyes toward her daughters. "Sorry," the agent muttered. "He's a jerk, but he also testified against Perez via closed circuit TV and behind a shielded screen. He was undercover as one of Perez's boys. If his cover had been blown, he'd be a head without a body, too."

"Okay," Laura Beth said, her voice laden with skepticism. "Then it's a coincidence he's got a big nose and just happens to be within five miles of my home."

"He's also with two other agents who would have overheard his conversation."

"Okay, okay." She held up her hands but looked toward McGill who had mentioned he thought a cop of some sort was dirty.

The local detective discreetly rubbed his index finger across his lips. Laura Beth realized Tanner had shared his thoughts about the case with her and Bruce without Pickering's knowledge.

"Fine," she said as the other three federal agents approached.

Pickering introduced them around. Luis Montoya met Laura Beth's warm brown eyes with glazed, watery ones. His beady eyes made his nose look even more disproportionate. His long, oily black hair pulled back in a ponytail and scruffy, unshaved face gave him the appearance of being a thug. The other two agents, Cline and Kilpatrick, seemed amicable enough. Pickering asked, "The boss send you?"

Kilpatrick nodded. "Only because he thought Luis might be able to shed some light on the case since he was around Perez for so long."

"And?" Pickering asked. The hostility was not lost on the local detective or Laura Beth, as frightened as she was. They gave each other a significant look.

Montoya replied in a silky southern drawl, "He's got somebody on his payroll. Your hitman is a cop, Pickering, a Fed."

"You?"

The chuckle from Montoya told Laura Beth the man did not like Pickering any more than Pickering liked him. "You'd like that, wouldn't you?"

"Okay, boys," Laura Beth said. "You can posture later. I don't care which of you is alpha dog, but I want my family protected."

"Which I will arrange, Mrs. Copeland," assured Pickering. "Let's get this show on the road. I'll call you as soon as I get things taken care of."

"Thanks." All law enforcement began to drift away. "Tanner," Laura Beth called. "Bruce asked if you might be able to stay until he gets home."

"Sure. This is out of my jurisdiction anyway, but I can sit with a friend. Let me check in to be certain I'm not needed in the office."

McGill stepped away to call in. Laura Beth escorted the federal agents to the door. Pickering held back. "I'll get a watch on this house." He glared over his shoulder.

Laura Beth patted the agent's arm with a petite hand. "Cut him some slack. I think he's been desensitized by being undercover. Part of him is still in that persona."

"You're too nice. It might get you killed."

Pickering walked to his car. McGill stood behind Laura Beth, his hand resting on top of the front door. "Not while I'm around."

Arms folded protectively across her chest, she turned her auburn head around and up to look into determined sapphire-blue eyes. "Thanks, Tanner."

The detective guided Laura Beth inside with a gentle hand on her elbow and closed the door with authority. "You gonna feed me while I babysit?"

The man's genuine smile of perfect white teeth put Laura Beth at ease. "Sure. Grilled cheese sandwiches, tomato soup, and fruit cocktail for lunch."

Both of them turned back as the sound of other cars grabbed their attention. A white Camry and a red Cobalt came to a stop. Laura Beth laughed. "They're late. With all the drama I forgot all about the Enterprise folks delivering the rental car."

7
A Watchful Eye

By the time Bruce arrived home, a deputy sheriff's car sat in his driveway. The doctor entered to see Tanner McGill sitting cross-legged in the floor playing *Candy Land* with his two daughters. His wife sat with her feet curled under her on the sofa pretending to read, but actually watching the detective deliberately lose a child's game.

The second her husband came into the room, Laura Beth skipped to him and greeted him with a kiss. He dipped his head toward their company. Laura Beth laughed. "He stayed until you got home as you asked."

"There's a deputy outside."

McGill stood and stretched to his full six-feet-two-inches. "Ladies, the man of the house is home, and I need to go to my home. I enjoyed our game."

Stacey and Tonya chorused, "'Bye, Mr. Tanner."

The detective stopped to shake hands with Bruce. He spoke in hushed tones so the children would be unable to hear. He did not want to frighten them any more than they already were. "Pickering has arranged surveillance. Either one of Penny's men or one of his will be outside until this guy is caught. Your house is out of my jurisdiction, but you might expect either Officer Dixon or me to put in an appearance. Perez was killed on *my* turf. I'll have y'all under a watchful eye."

"Thanks," said Bruce. "I feel better with someone I know taking care of this mess."

"You know Penny. She's a good sheriff."

"Yes, she is. Still, I don't know much about Pickering."

"I know he doesn't like one of the new guys," Laura Beth said.

McGill shrugged. "I sense bad blood there, but Pickering is a good guy. He wants to solve this mess, and he's loath to admit one of his own might be the bad guy."

"Thanks for staying," Bruce reiterated.

"Later. Call if anything weird happens." McGill left.

Bruce slipped his arms around his wife and moaned. "Should I feel jealous of his familiarity?"

"No." She knitted her brows together in consternation.

"Long day, baby. What's for supper?" He changed the subject quickly.

"Lemon pepper chicken, long-grain and wild rice, green beans, and peach cobbler."

"Sounds yummy."

~

Just before midnight as Bruce and Laura Beth got ready to turn in for the night, they saw the deputy leave and another vehicle take his place. "Who is it?" Laura Beth asked as she peeked over her husband's shoulder.

"Don't know."

"Is it Tanner?"

"No."

"Officer Dixon?"

"No. They can't officially stake us out."

The person stepped from the car and lit a cigarette. "Oh," Laura Beth grunted. "It's that Montoya fellow that Pickering doesn't like." She narrowed her eyes to slits. "He'd better not drop that butt on my driveway."

Bruce laughed. "You're worried about a cigarette butt when the man's here to protect you?"

She dipped her chin and looked through squinted eyes. "Maybe if Pickering liked him, I wouldn't be suspicious."

Bruce turned off the light and escorted his wife to bed. "If there are butts in the morning, we'll speak to him. Remember he has to stay awake out there."

"Maybe I should take him some coffee? Something to eat?"

"It's almost midnight, darling."

"So? He's got the graveyard shift. He needs nourishment." The stubborn redhead marched to the kitchen where she prepared a fresh pot of coffee, filled a thermos and made a plate of leftovers from supper.

Laura Beth walked outside and knocked on the window of the surveillance vehicle after she checked the ground for a cigarette butt. The security light provided adequate illumination to show the man had not dropped his trash on the ground. Laura Beth smiled.

Montoya lowered the window. "I didn't mean to wake you, ma'am," he said in a thick Texas twang.

"You didn't. We were just heading to bed. I thought you could use some coffee and food."

The agent gave her a half smile, and she noticed the scar in his cheek. "That's awfully kind of you." He extended his hands to take the offering. They shook. "I'll be here 'til morning. Thanks."

"No problem. Good night." She started inside but turned back. "Agent Montoya, what's this hostility between you and Agent Pickering?"

"You picked up on that, huh?"

"Yeah, it's kind of hard to miss. Yet, here you are guarding me."

"Pickering blames me for his son's death. We were partners and were ambushed. He died." He touched the scar in his cheek. "I lived."

"Pickering said you were undercover."

"I was. No more. I put the scum away that was responsible for Charlie's death."

"Perez?"

"Yes, ma'am." He ran a bony hand through the greasy black hair that hung below his shoulders, and then fished an elastic band from the pocket in his jeans, pulling the strands into a ponytail.

Laura Beth made a disapproving face at his choice of hairstyles.

He laughed softly and sardonically. "As soon as I can, I'm getting a haircut so I don't look so much like a greaser." He tapped his nose. "Big nose like you described, but it wasn't me. I swear."

"For some reason, I believe you. Good night."

~

The next morning Bruce called over his shoulder before he left at seven, "My competition is here."

"What?" asked Laura Beth.

"Tanner."

"You are being silly. He told you he'd be checking."

Tanner walked onto the low concrete wrap-around porch. "Thought I'd see how surveillance went last night. Pickering said he sent Montoya."

"He did," said Laura Beth. "And I talked to him. He's okay."

"Pickering has bad feelings toward him."

"He told me why."

McGill lifted his eyebrow in question. The woman shrugged. "It seems Pickering blames Montoya for his son's death."

"I see," mumbled McGill. "I think he mentioned they were partners. I knew the son had been killed in the line of duty."

"Apparently, Montoya was wounded. He has a deep scar on his face. And his hands shake too much to cut off someone's head."

The detective glanced at Bruce before he intoned, "So, are you a detective now?"

"No." Laura Beth folded her arms across her chest and puffed out her cheeks.

Tanner covered his mouth to keep from laughing.

"What?" she asked, her voice shrill.

"Uh-oh," muttered Bruce. "You've pissed her off, Tanner."

She huffed, "I just noticed how much his hands shook when he took the coffee and plate last night."

"You fed him?" asked Tanner in disbelief.

"Yes." Her auburn hair bounced as she gave her head a half-shake.

Bruce started laughing. "She's a mother hen."

"Oh, stop it!" She looked the detective in the eye. "Why do his hands shake so badly? Not good for holding a gun."

"Cocaine withdrawal," replied McGill. "Undercover he had to use. He's clean but drying out. Residual tremors are not uncommon."

"Is that why he's so thin?"

"Probably, but you're fattening him up."

"I have to get to the hospital in Jackson today," Bruce said with a chuckle. He kissed his wife soundly. "I love you."

"I love you more."

"I love you most."

The doctor left for work. Laura Beth turned to Tanner McGill. "Would you like some fattening?"

The detective laughed loudly, prompting the deputy who had replaced Montoya to poke his head out the car window. "No thanks. I already had breakfast. I gotta get to the station. I just wanted to check on you."

"I'm glad you stopped by. Will you let me know if you discover anything?"

"You bet." Tanner left with a wave to the deputy. He stopped beside the patrol car. "Let me know what she serves you for lunch."

The deputy looked perplexed but enjoyed fried catfish nuggets, tater tots, and coleslaw for lunch.

~

Just after serving the deputy lunch, Laura Beth was drawn to her front door by the sounds of an altercation with a woman screeching, "Get your hands off me!"

Laura Beth jerked the front door open to see a tall gray-haired woman resisting the deputy's detaining of her. "Madeleine?" said Laura Beth.

The older woman turned toward Laura Beth. "Tell this oaf we're friends. He says I'm not on the list."

"What list?"

The deputy, without releasing his grip on Madeleine, replied, "Dr. Copeland gave us a list of people who were permitted to pass."

"He didn't ask me," Laura Beth said. "Add Madeleine Becker to your list. She's my friend."

The deputy let go. "Yes, ma'am."

"Oh, and show me the list so I can be sure *my* friends are on there."

"Yes, ma'am." The deputy returned to his car and brought a printed list of names. He looked sheepish. Madeleine still smoothed wrinkles from her rumpled pant suit. "Sorry, ma'am," said the deputy.

"You were doing your job," Madeleine acknowledged grudgingly.

Laura Beth took the list and held her hand out to Madeleine. "Pen."

The older woman reached into her purse and handed the younger one a pen. Laura Beth added several names to the list and handed it back to the deputy. "Add these, and we're good to go."

"Yes, ma'am."

"I appreciate your watchful eye. Do you need anything else?"

"Not right now. The meal was delicious."

She nodded. "Madeleine, come in. What brings you here?" The man went back to the cruiser, and the ladies went inside.

"Doug Blanchard told us about finding that dead woman and that you've been a target of this madman. I had to check on you. I didn't know you would be surrounded by storm troopers."

"Sit down. Tea?"

"Yes, please."

Laura Beth brought two glasses of iced tea. "I'm afraid after the last few days I need the protection. The man broke into the house and somehow bypassed the security system. He left a dead rat in the cradle in the nursery." She sat beside the other woman on the sofa.

"Good heavens! After he ran you off the road?"

"I think he was coming from the house when I was headed home. He took advantage of the situation. I discovered the rat the next morning."

"Well, honey, if you need a place to hide out, come to me. I have a list, too, at the gate to my neighborhood." She patted the younger woman's leg. "Where are your girls?"

"Napping."

"I was hoping to meet them."

"Hang around about an hour. How is the census-taking going?"

"All right. I think I've done one of every kind now, including an in-mover. I haven't had any real complications. I hate getting a proxy though. The main office keeps changing the rules."

"How?"

"Well, you know at first they said try three times before using a proxy?"

Laura Beth nodded.

"Now, we have to try six times, and then they send the EQs back because the proxy can't give all the information. I know I'm getting paid, but this is wasting my tax dollars big time." She set her glass on the coaster with force.

Laura Beth laughed. "I guess it's good I'm putting work on hold because I would unload on somebody."

"Poor Doug. He gets the worst of it."

"Doug?"

"Blanchard."

"I know who Doug is, but since when are you on a first name basis with him?"

"Since he took me to dinner and brought flowers."

"Oh, my God! You're dating?"

"And we have a movie date Friday." The two women began to chatter and giggle like teenagers.

~

Madeleine stayed for dinner and enjoyed a visit with her former doctor. When the older woman left, a different deputy was on duty. Laura Beth cut her husband a reproachful look.

Bruce held up his hands in surrender. "Sorry I didn't run the list by you first."

"You deserve a beating."

"Let's put the girls to bed and you can use those silk scarves to tie me up. Give me one of your tongue lashings."

She bit her index finger coquettishly. "You wash the dishes and I'll bathe the girls. We have a date in an hour."

~

At midnight, Luis Montoya relieved the deputy who was watching the house. Fifteen minutes later a Camaro parked behind the Impala Montoya used. The agent got out with his hand on his weapon.

Officer Marge Dixon stepped from the Chevy. "Take it easy, big boy," she said.

"Officer Dixon?"

"Yeah. My boss told me to check out the situation."

"The situation or me?"

"Six of one, half dozen of another."

"Not really. I'm a good agent. I'm not a killer."

"Get defensive, why don't you?" The tall, big-boned blonde with hair cropped to only an inch long leaned against her blood-red car.

"Nice wheels," said Montoya.

"Thanks. Got it at auction for a song." She eyed the agent. "I see you washed the oil slick."

He ran a hand across his hair, still long and in a ponytail. "Gonna cut it soon."

"Naa. Leave it."

"I hate it." He leaned against the car beside the woman.

Dixon shrugged. "Your hair, but why do you hate it?"

"It makes me look like a thug."

"Wasn't that the point?"

"Operative word—was."

"Gotcha. What does your woman think of it?"

"Don't have one. A wife or girlfriend and undercover don't mix."

"Thought you were leaving undercover."

"I am." The man let his eyes rove over the woman beside him. "Do you like long hair on your partner?"

"Partner?" She pushed up from the car. "As in the person who rides shotgun while I work or lover?" Montoya heard Dixon's teeth snap shut.

"Umm. Hey!" He raised his hands as if in surrender. "Don't get pissed at me. Some of the guys just said..."

"I'm a dyke? Or ice queen?"

"Never mind." He started back to his car.

The officer called after him, "What do you think, Montoya? Which am I?"

"I don't care."

As he put his hand on the car door, another vehicle approached. The agent walked briskly back to the officer. Dixon whispered. "I'm out of jurisdiction. I have no authority here."

A pizza delivery car pulled beside the Camaro. "Is this the Copeland residence?" asked the driver, a blonde bombshell with breasts overflowing the uniform.

"Who needs to know?" asked Montoya.

"I'm supposed to deliver this here pizza to a Luis Montoya at this address, if it's the right one. Agent Pickering thought you might be hungry."

"Pickering sent me food?" He glanced at Dixon who shrugged.

The delivery person's ponytail bobbed when she nodded. "It's already paid for, tip and all. It's a supreme."

Montoya held his gun at the ready. He indicated with the barrel. "Open the box."

The girl opened the box and both law enforcers looked at the pizza. Dixon whispered, "She can't be hiding a weapon as tight as those clothes are."

"Pickering hates me," Montoya whispered back.

"You *are* watching the house on the graveyard shift. Maybe he had a change of heart, a little. It's hot, and it smells great."

Montoya lowered the box lid and took the food. The delivery girl turned to leave. "Enjoy." Ponytail and boobs bounced as she got into the car and left.

The agent holstered his weapon. Dixon put her hands on her hips. "Share and I'll tell you whether I'm a dyke or an ice queen."

Montoya laughed. "My car or yours?"

Dixon's brows shot to her hair line. "You're not dripping tomato sauce and cheese in my baby."

The man indicated with his head for her to follow. Inside the Impala with the windows down, each took a slice of pizza. Around a mouthful, Montoya said, "So which are you?"

Dixon swallowed. "Neither. I'm straight as an arrow. I'm hesitant to get involved with anyone I work with because I was married to a cop, highway patrol. He was killed in the line of duty. Routine stop turned deadly. I have a four-year old daughter. She was barely six months when her father died." She tapped her head. "The man cut is because she got lice at pre-school and shared with me."

Montoya snickered.

Dixon dipped her chin. "Have you ever had that scourge? I had shoulder-length hair I pulled up for work. Hers was to her butt. Combing that mess to get rid of nits was a *nightmare*. We both have super short hair now. If it ever happens again, won't be much to comb through. This pizza is good."

"Yeah. I'm still shocked Pickering sent it."

"So? Is it true you were his kid's partner and he got killed?"

"Yeah. I think Ed blames me. That's why he treats me so bad."

"Maybe he's still mourning."

Montoya shrugged and rubbed the back of his neck. He stretched his eyes.

Dixon yawned. "Shit," she muttered, looking at the man beside her as his head drooped. She fumbled with her cell. It slid to the floor. She slumped onto Montoya's shoulder.

.8

Car Swap

As the sun topped the trees, savage pounding on the driver's side door awakened Officer Dixon and Agent Montoya. "Wake up! What the hell?" bellowed Tanner McGill, his blue eyes blazing like the hottest fire. He wrenched the door open.

Still groggy, Dixon mumbled, "I can explain, Boss."

"You better. And everyone in that house"— He pointed with a sharp finger in the direction of the house—"had best be okay."

Montoya tapped the pizza box. "The pizza. Someone drugged the pizza."

Tanner asked, "Where did the pizza come from?"

Finally awake, Montoya said, "Delivery. The girl said Pickering sent it. I shared with Dixon. Don't blame her."

"Don't blame Montoya!" Dixon snapped. "He thought his boss was being a nice guy."

"Shit!" McGill stomped a few paces from the car, fist to his mouth, and came back. "Describe her."

Dixon began, "Bottled-blonde. Hair in a ponytail. Five-feet, eight-inches. Mid-twenties."

With his hands extended in front of him, Montoya added, "Knockers out to here." Dixon scowled at him. "Probably fake," the agent added for some unknown reason.

McGill ran a hand through his hair, grabbing a handful at the crown of his head as if pulling out his own hair. "It might interest you two to know that just after midnight last night a seventeen-year-old high-school kid delivered a supreme pizza to one Putzy Whetting, stripper, bottled-blonde, mid-twenties, five-foot-eight, 38 double D silicone implants, missing—she never reported for work on the morning shift. We can't file a missing person's report on her until she's been gone forty-eight hours because she's an adult. The boy was hit with a TASER as he gawked at the woman's boobs. He came to, near the pizza place. He was wearing only his underwear. He was not robbed. A crisp twenty lay on his car seat."

"Wow!" exclaimed Dixon.

"I'm not done," growled McGill, shaking his head with slow deliberation. "That's not the news I came to share, but it apparently has bearing on this case. When we find our hitman, we can add assaulting two officers."

"Why *did* you come out here this morning?" asked Montoya.

"I promised the Copelands I'd let them know if anything new developed. Walk up with me. I'll tell everyone at the same time, if they're okay; and they had *better* be." He glared at Dixon. He pointed sharply then clenched his fist, bringing it to his mouth. He turned an acute military one-eighty and went toward the house. He stopped and walked around the black Mercedes and the white rented Camry, running his hands over the doors and checking the locks. *Looks normal.*

The two sheepish law enforcement officers trailed McGill onto the porch. He rang the bell. Bruce Copeland opened the door. "You're early this morning."

"I have news. May we come in?"

"Sure. Laura Beth just started a pot of coffee. Want some?"

"Yes," said Dixon, rubbing the crick out of her neck. She suddenly felt strong, yet gentle, pressure from Montoya's thumb on the muscle that was giving her fits. "Thanks," she whispered.

"Sorry about the pizza."

"Not your fault."

"What's wrong with pizza?" asked Bruce. "It's one of my favorite vices."

McGill took a deep breath. "Apparently someone drugged a pizza and brought it to these two…numbskulls. It knocked them out. But y'all aren't hurt. Maybe it was a tactic to show how close he could get to the house even with cops watching."

"Damn it," muttered Bruce. He led the three officers to the breakfast nook where he kissed his wife's cheek. "Got enough for everybody?"

"I can make more." She poured five mugs of coffee, pointed out the cream and sugar, and started a second pot.

As they sat around the dinette, McGill began. He told them about the pizza boy and took a gulp of coffee before he delivered the news he had come to convey. "It seems we have a car swap. Firefighters responded early this morning to a car burning on the highway. The charred remains of a woman were found inside the burnt-out Escalade."

"Oh, my God!" Laura Beth slapped her hands over her mouth.

"You think it's Miss Whetting?" asked Dixon.

"Probably. She was seen with a brawny man with a prominent nose. We're trying to get an artist to draw what the other strippers saw, but the ladies don't agree. And we're getting a court order for the surveillance video in front of the club. I think our guy charmed her, used her, and killed her."

"But he's driving a different car?" asked Bruce.

"It would seem so."

"That makes my decision firm." He gave his wife an authoritative glower. "I'm delivering the Camry to the dealership and picking up the Jag. Baby, you can use the Mercedes today."

"Fine. I won't argue."

"Excuse me. I need to make a call," said Bruce. He called his office.

~

Bruce prepared to leave for Jackson to pick up Laura Beth's car. Montoya and Dixon sauntered back to their vehicles as a deputy pulled in for a turn at watching the house. The two informed the deputy of the latest events.

McGill stood on the porch with Bruce and Laura Beth. Bruce kissed his wife. "I've rescheduled my morning appointments for this afternoon. If I leave right now"—He glanced at his watch— "It's half past seven. I should be in Jackson in about two hours. I'll be back as soon as I get the car, grab lunch with you and see patients beginning at one. It'll put me late getting home though," he informed her.

"Okay. Drive safely. You don't *have* to hurry."

Copeland turned to McGill. "Are you staying?"

The detective shook his head and pointed. "Penny's man is here, and I'm taking the leftover pizza to be analyzed."

"You think it was just a test to show how vulnerable we are?" asked Laura Beth.

McGill looked around and shrugged. "I don't see anything out of place. The cars were locked. Nothing looks odd."

"I need to hit the road," said Bruce. He kissed Laura Beth again. "I love you."

"I love you more."

"I love you most."

McGill chuckled. "Is that a routine?"

"Sort of," confessed Bruce. "We've always done it. Whoever says, 'I love you,' first gets the last word."

McGill laughed outright. "I'd bet you never actually get the last word."

"Not funny," said Laura Beth.

Bruce stepped off the porch and slid behind the steering wheel of the Camry. He adjusted the seat to fit his longer legs. He waved.

BOOM!

The car erupted in flames before it ever cranked. Debris flew in all directions.

"Bruce!" screamed Laura Beth as she bolted toward the blazing vehicle.

McGill restrained her. "No!"

The other three law enforcement officers rushed to the burning vehicle, the deputy lugging a fire extinguisher. Dixon summoned emergency personnel immediately.

The three battled the blaze, dousing the flames. Montoya jerked the driver's door open, burning his hand severely. Dixon stood shoulder to shoulder with him. She gave Montoya a doubtful expression but checked for a pulse on the charred body of Bruce Copeland. "He never knew what hit him," she said. "It's better that way." She shook her head toward her boss as firefighters and an ambulance roared into the driveway.

Stacey and Tonya Copeland emerged from the door of the house to see the smoldering car and McGill holding their mother in a vise-grip. "Where's Daddy?" screamed Stacey.

Laura Beth gulped, "Oh, God! It should have been me. He was trying to kill me."

"Stop," scolded McGill gently. "Think about your kids and the one inside you. Bruce would not want you blaming yourself."

Laura Beth collapsed into the detective's arms.

9
Safekeeping

As the ambulance left, Ed Pickering pulled in. "Somebody better start talking," he bellowed the second he stepped from his car. His face contorted at the acrid stench of the burning rubber and his eyes smarted from the lingering smoke.

McGill indicated for Dixon to take Laura Beth. He led Pickering to the side as crime scene investigators and the bomb squad appeared. He told the agent about the pizza. Pickering turned red in the face with rage and started toward Montoya.

A hand firmly on the agent's shoulder, "Stop," McGill said. "Montoya and Dixon believed you sent it. Obviously, the asshole rigged the car as everyone slept. He's killed two people in the last twelve hours. I think it's time to pay a visit to Perez and see if you can get anything out of him. He won't be happy with his hitman being so sloppy."

"He won't care. He's behind bars for the next thirty years. He'll just find a way to send a different assassin after this hitman." He lowered his voice. "Besides, Ninja Man told me on the phone that Perez didn't hire him."

"You believe him?"

Pickering nodded.

"Ninja Man?"

"The sword." The agent shrugged. "It just makes me think of ninja warriors."

"You could be right." The detective plunged his hands into his pants pockets. "Laura Beth is a mess now. When whoever is in charge finds out the wrong person was in the car, he'll try again." He breathed a ragged sigh. "I looked both cars over. I didn't see a thing. I worked bomb disposal in Afghanistan. What's wrong with me?"

"Now you stop. You didn't see anything amiss." Pickering put a finger against McGill's chest, stopping short of poking him. "We need to get Mrs. Copeland to a safe house." Pickering looked toward Montoya. "You sure he was asleep?"

"Ed, the man is a good cop. Cut him some slack. He needs a doctor. His hands are burned."

"You take him. I've got to arrange a safe house."

"Ed, he didn't kill your son."

The older agent scowled. McGill left him to stew and took the younger agent to have his hands attended.

Dixon followed, her mind wondering. *Pissing contest, Tanner. You and Pickering need to get a grip and stop fighting over who's in control.* She practically laughed. *Actually, if Penny had made it here before either of you left, she'd show whose turf you're on.*

"Boss! Hold up she called."

"What?"

"Don't get short with me. I know I screwed up, but listen. The hitman wouldn't have known Bruce would take the car AND if he's been watching, which I suspect, he would have known Laura Beth wouldn't leave the house until mid-morning, if at all. I'm thinking only the car was supposed to go boom, not a person."

"You have to be shitting me. Is this blonde logic."

"Screw you. You happen to be blond, too." She stormed off.

Tanner mused on his assistant's theory.

~

Several hours later, McGill burst into the office Pickering was using. "Where is she?" he demanded.

"Safe house. But she is pitching a fit. She's mad about not being able to give her husband a funeral. And I had to send someone to tell his parents. I think she could become violent."

"Can you blame her? Maybe if you let me talk to her, I can calm her. Did you assure her the morgue will hold Bruce until all this is over? My God, man! She saw her husband incinerated this morning. She's in shock, and she's pregnant."

McGill plopped into the chair in front of the desk. Pickering leaned forward and placed his elbows on the desk. "Do you think I'm heartless? Of course, I told her we'd hold off on a funeral. And I made her go see her doctor before I whisked her away. Her girls are with her friend, Madeleine. They could use a father figure right now. I haven't told anyone else where the girls are. This son of a bitch would go after her kids. He's cold and cruel. If I think you should know where she is, I'll tell you. Right now, I want as few people as possible to know. Go visit the kids. Their grandparents, Laura Beth's folks, will be coming for them tonight to take them to the Coast."

"I'm not so sure you're right about whoever blew up the car. Dixon had a theory that's not *all* water. Maybe only the car was supposed to blow up." He told Pickering what his assistant had said. McGill bumped his hands against the arms of the chair and rubbed his palms back and forth as Pickering just stared at him.

With the dead silence, Tanner finally said, "Yeah, okay. I'll check on the girls. This newest development has Penny Ulmer right in here with us. Does she know where you took Laura Beth?"

"Nope. How's my agent?"

"Montoya will be out of commission for a couple of weeks. He burned himself badly trying to get Bruce out."

"You don't think he's the inside man, do you?"

"No, I don't. I think he's young and trying desperately to win your approval."

"You don't pull your punches, do you, McGill?"

"No. I call 'em like I see 'em."

Pickering heaved deeply. "In my mind, I know it wasn't his fault Charlie got killed. He almost died, too. I guess I just need someone to blame."

"It's part of grieving, Ed." He leaned forward with his elbows on his knees. "Luis is grieving for his partner—his friend. Maybe together, you can overcome the bad blood." He sat back and locked his blue eyes onto the agent's honey-brown ones. "Was Perez ultimately responsible? Didn't Luis help bring him down?"

"Yeah." The older man nodded with some reluctance. "And now the bastard or someone in his corner is after an innocent woman."

"You know, I bet our assassin didn't count on Dixon showing up last night. He wanted this to look as if Montoya was the guilty party. Dixon corroborates everything. And he killed his unwitting accomplice. He's getting sloppy. Maybe. Something just feels really off here."

"I suppose. I have agents going over film footage from the strip club and the apartment complex. Maybe with Mrs. Copeland's sketch we can put a face together."

McGill stood. "Right then. Keep me in the loop. I'm going to look in on two scared little girls."

~

At the hospital, Marge Dixon sat in a chair by the bed where Luis Montoya slept after allowing the doctors to give him one dose of morphine. He had argued that he didn't want anything remotely addictive. She bounced her four-year-old daughter on her lap. Luis opened his eyes. "I've died and gone to Heaven," he mumbled. "I see two angels."

"Hey," said Marge. "They're cutting you loose if you have a place to go."

"Guess I'll be here then." He drifted off for another moment before murmuring, "I only have a hotel room that the agency is paying for."

"That's why I'm here." She looked down at her daughter. "This is Deannie. Meet Mr. Montoya."

"Hi," said the little girl.

Marge continued, "I'm taking you home with me. You need a safe house for a couple of weeks, and I'm on suspension with pay for two weeks. That's what I get for sharing a pizza with a greaser."

"Haircut coming." The man chuckled sleepily.

"Keep it. I kind of like the bad-boy image."

He opened his eyes as far as they would go. A smile flickered across his face.

A knock startled both of them. Ed Pickering entered with a pizza in hand. He held it up. "This one really is from me."

"I might choke on pizza," said Montoya.

"Thought so. How about you, little lady? Would you like a slice of pepperoni pizza?" He looked at the little girl who looked up at her mother. Marge nodded.

Deannie took a slice of pizza and said, "Thank you."

"You're welcome. Montoya, where are you gonna go from here?"

A smirk played around Montoya's lips. "I'm going home with two angels."

Pickering looked at Dixon and nodded. "Good call." He turned back to the agent. "I just wanted to let you know, I believe you. You're a good man, and I'm glad you're on my team."

Stunned speechless, the younger man nodded. Pickering left without further ado.

~

Tanner knocked on Madeleine Becker's door. She opened cautiously. "How did you get in the gate?"

He flashed his badge. "Not good," said Madeleine. "If the killer is a cop, he could do the same thing."

"You have a point," McGill agreed. "But I'm not a killer, and I think the girls could use a friend right now."

Madeleine opened the door and let the detective in. "Stacey hasn't stopped crying. Tonya just blinks. I don't think she understands."

Tanner walked into Madeleine's living room. Both girls ran to him upon sight. He knelt to be on their level and held one in each arm. Stacey wept, "My daddy's dead, Mr. Tanner."

"I know, sweetheart. He's in Heaven now."

The younger girl buried her face in the detective's shoulder. He kissed the top of her head. "It's okay. Your grandparents are coming later to get you."

"Where's Mommy?" asked Stacey.

"Agent Pickering put her somewhere safe."

"But our house wasn't safe. Is anywhere safe?" The five-year-old sounded grown.

"Oh, sweetheart. You're too young to think like that. I'll make sure your mommy is safe." He lifted his head to look at Madeleine.

The gray-haired lady gave him a fleeting smile. "Girls, let me talk to Detective McGill. Go back and watch TV." Strains from *The Sound of Music* floated on the air.

Holding hands, the girls obeyed. "How?" asked Madeleine in hushed tones once the girls were out of earshot. "How will you keep Laura Beth safe?"

"I don't know."

McGill stayed until the grandparents picked up the girls. He gave them his card should they need him. He turned to the woman who had lost a friend that day. "I don't know what to do, Mrs. Becker."

She patted the man's arm. "You're going to have supper with me."

10
An Inside Job

For three days Laura Beth did nothing but sleep and cry. Agent Alice Kilpatrick came from the bedroom where her charge lay curled in the fetal position. She set the tray of untouched food on the kitchen counter. "She's gonna make herself sick," she said to Agent Cline.

Cline ran an ebony hand over his slick head. "She's mourning." The tall, muscular man stood and walked to the door where Laura Beth hibernated. He knocked softly. "Mrs. Copeland, may I come in?"

"Okay." Her voice quaked.

Cline came in and sat on the edge of the bed. He patted her back as he would a child. "Listen. I know your heart is breaking, but Pickering said you're pregnant. Not eating and not taking care of yourself isn't good for the baby."

"Every time I try, it gets stuck in my throat and I want to vomit. I need Bruce." She let loose with another round of tears.

"If I make you some soup, will you at least try to eat for Bruce's baby?"

Laura Beth sat up. "Bruce's baby." She wiped her eyes and blew her nose on a tissue she held. "Yes. I need to start thinking like that. Do you think I should call him Bruce?"

"If you want to."

"Bruce didn't want a junior, but maybe his middle name should be Bruce."

"Now that's more positive thinking. I'll make you that soup."

~

Laura Beth returned her own tray to the kitchen sink. "Well, looks who's moving." Agent Cline smiled at the woman he was assigned to protect. "Feeling a little better?"

"A little." She sighed. "How's Agent Montoya?"

"Fine, I guess. We can't call to check since we have to keep our location secret."

"I can't call my girls?"

"No, sweetheart. It's too risky right now."

The door to the extended-stay-hotel apartment Pickering had secured opened. Kilpatrick struggled to bring in several grocery bags. Cline rushed to help his partner. "Thanks," she said.

The woman looked toward the kitchen. "Good to see you up and about."

Laura Beth nodded. "You got enough for an army."

"I don't know how long we'll be here, hon." The agent began putting away the items she had bought.

"Let me help," said Laura Beth. "Y'all want me to cook? I'm a good cook."

"Sure thing. I hate cooking." Kilpatrick grinned.

The new widow smiled sadly. "If I keep busy, I'll do better."

"I gotcha," replied Kilpatrick. "But maybe you should shower and get cleaned up first."

Self-consciously, Laura Beth touched her tangled hair. "I must look frightful."

"No," said Cline back on the sofa. "You look like a woman who's been through hell. But I bet a shower would make you feel better. Then, you can dazzle me, if not my partner, with your culinary skills."

"You've got it." She left to bathe and change clothes.

The two agents exchanged nods. "She'll be okay," said Cline.

~

Laura Beth stood in the steamy shower and let the sting of the pelting water ease her weary mind. The coconut-lime scented bath gel and shampoo offered refreshing and stimulating aroma. As she turned off the nozzle, she heard a resounding knock on the door to the apartment, followed by calm, as if familiar, voices. *Pickering must have sent another agent to relieve either Cline or Kilpatrick, or both* she thought. *Too bad. I sort of like them.*

She toweled her hair and slipped into the terrycloth robe that hung on the door. She pulled the soft, fluffy material up to her neck. She leaned her ear closer to the bathroom door when she heard a distinct thump then a bellow that sounded like Cline and another hard thud. That was followed by what sounded like the door being flung open and hitting the wall and an unearthly male scream.

With her brow creased deeply, Laura Beth opened the bathroom door. The adjoining bedroom was dark as the orange and magenta of the sunset showed dimly through the opaque drapes. Laura Beth started toward the bedside table lamp as the bedroom door flew open.

Silhouetted in the twilight shadows stood a bulky form with a bulbous nose. An open trench coat billowed out as the man marched toward Laura Beth, a long, slightly curved sword raised in the air. A dark substance dribbled down the blade.

A scratchy voice asked, "Is anyone in here besides you?"

Laura Beth started back toward the bathroom, but the intruder overtook her with ease. The man grabbed her arm and flung her onto the bed. He raised the blade, and it seemed to disappear into his back. Laura Beth aimed her kick for the groin, connecting with denim. The man groaned but barely moved.

Terror stricken, she kicked wildly for any part of her assailant's body she could find. Inching back on the bed, she felt for her purse she knew was on the other nightstand.

The man dropped one hand to his side. "In all honesty, I don't want to do a damned thing to you, but I have my orders." He pinned the struggling woman. "Listen to me if you want to live. You might be a little spitfire, but you are no match for what you're up against. Do you want your head shipped to Pickering?" *I hate this. Cooperate and maybe I can get you out of this alive.*

"Get off me, you son of a bitch!" Laura Beth tried to scream, but the heavy man clamped his hand over her mouth. She wiggled and writhed. Twisting her head back and forth, she managed to bite the fleshier part of the man's hand just below his fingers.

He jerked his hand back. "Damn! You are a little tigress." He sucked on the place she had bitten but kept his other forearm across her chest. "If you stop fighting me..."

Flailing her hand back, her fingertips felt the strap of her purse. She hooked her finger in the strap and pulled the bag closer. Grasping the straps, she swung with all her might, catching the man against his head and spilling the contents of the handbag.

"Damn you, woman!" he growled. "What you got in there—bricks?"

He relieved his pressure against her for a second to rub the side of his head, and she felt around the contents from her purse. Her hand landed on the body spritz she carried. She flipped the cap off with her thumbnail and sprayed the man in the face.

The would-be assassin bawled and rubbed his eyes for the alcohol worked as well as pepper spray. Laura Beth managed to roll from the man's grasp and sprinted toward the door, pausing only long enough to snatch her cell phone from among the items scattered on the mattress. The impact of falling had caused the screen to light up.

An unstoppable scream escaped Laura Beth's throat when she entered the sitting area of the suite. The bitter smell of iron assaulted her nose. Both Cline and Kilpatrick lay in pools of blood, heads separated from bodies with one smooth swing of a crazy man's blade. Near them lay another headless body, a face she had never seen, but this body's hands also held a long blade. *The thuds were their bodies hitting the ground* ran through Laura Beth's frenzied mind.

Agent Cline lay closest to the door. Laura Beth squatted quickly and snagged his sidearm. "You bitch!" she heard in the bedroom doorway. "I'm trying to keep you alive," he muttered.

The words fell on deaf ears.

Seeing the glint of steel in the waning light, Laura Beth darted out the door. She was met by a deserted parking lot except for the agents' car and the one the other dead man and the man inside must have driven. It dawned on her she had no idea where she was, and nobody was supposed to know where to find her. The lunatic coming after her was an inside man. He was an agent.

Laura Beth slid the gun into firing position. She fired without aiming toward the motel. "Argh!" She heard behind her. "I am not looking forward to watching you die. Do you really want that baby you're carrying to die? I can make sure that doesn't happen." *Damn! She's one determined chick. She doesn't scare. I really thought fear would paralyze her.*

"Oh, hell no!" Laura Beth mumbled, and she fired again before she darted into what appeared to be a thicket. From there, she ran, oblivious to the thorns in her bare feet or the briars slashing at her calves.

She could still hear the ox behind her, bulling his way through underbrush. "Damn it," she muttered. "This robe just has to be white."

Realizing she still held her cell phone in her left hand, she scrolled until she found the number she wanted. She hit dial and kept running.

"Hello?"

"Madeleine! Help me. He killed the agents that were with me."

"Laura Beth? Where are you, honey?"

"I have no idea. I'm running through some woods, but he's hot on my trail."

Laura Beth fired the gun again in the general direction of the labored breathing she heard.

"What was that?" shrieked Madeleine.

"I took Agent Cline's gun. I'm just shooting in the dark." She took a breath. "I see a road."

"Road sign?"

Laura Beth looked around furtively until she spotted a small blue sign. "County 33, near an old extended-stay motel."

"Gus's Goulash."

"What? Gus's?"

"Do you see any buildings?"

"No, but I smell food."

"Follow your nose. You'll come up on a mom-and-pop restaurant, Gus's Gas and Goulash. I'm certain of it. Just walk right in."

"Madeleine, I only have on a bathrobe."

"Just walk right in."

Laura Beth gasped and flattened herself to the ground as her pursuer came parallel with her only a hundred yards away. A log truck rumbled by. An old car came by a minute later. A pickup with several boys riding in the back slowed as the driver saw the phantom in a black trench coat near the shoulder of the road. The truck stopped. "You lost, mister?" asked the boy in the passenger seat.

"Bugger off!"

"You got it." The driver pulled away.

Oh, stay. Oh, stay. The woman in hiding begged silently.

The black trench coat swished just above her head as Laura Beth slid into a mound of leaves. She could feel bugs crawling on her, but she bit her lip to remain quiet, drawing the metallic taste of blood. The stench of decaying leaves filled her nostrils. Overwhelming nausea hit. She swallowed back the bile.

After a few minutes with oaths of assured pain and death, the man headed back toward the hotel. Laura Beth saw a flicker of light as the man must have pulled out a cell phone.

~

"Who the hell is this?" a female voice asked.

"Somebody you need to listen to."

"How'd you get this phone?"

"Let's just say your man needed help. This assignment is getting totally out of hand."

"Where's McCormick?"

"Dead." *I took him out, you nutcase. I think I've got you fingered though. I have to end this.*

"I need a name."

"So do I."

"I guess this is a stalemate, but I'll find you if you're willing. Same deal I gave McCormick. If you can't do the job, I'll find someone who can. Then you will be of no use. You will have outlived your purpose. You're on your own. Am I making myself clear?"

"Crystal. I'll be in touch." The man shut his phone. "Cunt. I'd love to take off your head." He climbed into a black Charger and flipped open a different phone.

"Mosely," a man said.

"McCormick is dead, and I've lost the Copeland woman."

"What do you mean?"

"She's one hell of a little lady. But I have a number for you. It's probably untraceable, but I can tell you this much—your infiltrator is a woman. She's pretty much hired me now."

"Give me the number."

The number in his boss's hands, the man cranked his car thinking, *I'm realizing more and more this job's not on the up-and-up. I don't trust you, bitch—not one iota. If you're the deep-cover spy, I think I've finally got you. And I will do whatever I have to do to keep that little momma safe—Little Momma. Yeah, that's your name from now on.*

A smile flickered across his face, softening hard features.

~

Laura Beth turned on the turbo as she raced the way the truck of boys had gone. A quarter mile down the road, headlights blinded her. Her heart threatened to burst from her chest as she tried to tell herself the killer had not had time to get back to his car. She waved her arms frantically. The pickup full of teenage boys stopped.

"Lady, are you okay?" asked the driver.

"Help," she panted, out of breath. "That man."

"Was he after you?"

She nodded. The passenger jumped out and into the back with the other four boys. "Get in, lady. Where do you want me to take you?" the driver asked.

Laura Beth climbed into the passenger seat. "Gus's," she managed to wheeze out.

A boy sat between her and the driver. He looked down. "Are you packing, lady?"

She nodded again. "He tried to kill me. He killed the agents who were supposed to be protecting me and some other guy. I

took one of their guns. He threatened to rip my baby out of me."
She covered her face with her hands and started to sob.

The boy fumbled for some napkins in a cup holder and
handed them to her. "You're safe now. Get her to Gus's, Rod.
Then call the sheriff."

11
A Foul Weather Friend

At the packed little café, Laura Beth headed straight to the restroom. She reached in the pocket of the robe for the phone but found only lint. *Damn! It must've fallen out in the leaves.* She still had the nine-millimeter. *God, please let Madeleine come anyway.*

The group of boys sat in the back of the facility near a jukebox and a pool table, just out from the hallway where the restrooms were located. A soft knock on the door made Laura Beth hold her breath. The voice of the boy who had sat in the middle in the truck seat said, "Hey, lady, I got you a pair of jeans and a t-shirt from Gus's daughter. She's a little chunky, so the pants will probably fit you. If not, leave 'em unsnapped and the shirt is big enough to cover you up." A hand holding the clothes snaked through the door.

Laura Beth took the clothes. "Thanks."

"Are you hungry or thirsty? You want a Coke?"

"A Coke would be great."

"What kind?"

A smile flickered across the scared woman's face at the thought of all carbonated beverages being "Coke" in the Deep South. "Real Coke," she answered.

"You got it. The sheriff is on her way." The boy left the door.

Laura Beth changed into the borrowed clothes. Numerous welts from fire ant bites covered her thighs. The stiff denim irritated the bites and the scratches all along her calves. Even with the added waistline of pregnancy, she surmised the young man was being nice when he described the owner as "chunky." The jeans were loose in the waist. She took the dirty belt from the robe and threading it through the belt loops, cinched the pants to fit. The shirt hung almost to her knees and covered her well, which was good as she placed the gun in the small of her back inside the waistband of the jeans. She looked at her bare feet. *Oh well. It's the South. It's okay to go barefoot in early May.* She furrowed her brow. *Was that fool really wearing a trench coat? Pretty conspicuous if he's trying to hide.*

As Laura Beth started out the opening of the hallway toward where the group of boys sat, a brawny man about six feet wearing black jeans, a black western shirt, a black cowboy hat, and black cowboy boots entered. His nose took up half his face. The tail end of a snake medallion glinted silver on a chain at the man's throat. Laura Beth faded into the shadows.

The boy who had brought the clothes saw her and raised the Coke in the air. She shook her head vigorously and pointed. The boy looked over his shoulder as the man took a seat at the lunch counter rather than a booth or table.

The young man left their table and pulled Laura Beth to the door of the men's room. "You sure that's him? It was awfully dark. I ain't sure that's the guy on the road. He ain't wearin' the trench coat."

"Wouldn't that look funny as hot as it is?"

"Yeah, it would. You sure though?" The boy peered over the woman's head. "He's eatin'. Got a bowl of goulash."

"I'm not certain, but the guy had a huge nose and I know he had on jeans. I felt them when I kicked him in the nuts."

The boy snickered. "You a feisty lady."

She shrugged. "The man that broke into my house wore cowboy boots. Big nose, boots, stranger—too much coincidence to feel safe." She looked over her shoulder and tugged the boy's arm. "That's the lady coming to get me."

The boy nodded. "I got you covered. What's your name?"

"Laura Beth Copeland."

"I got you covered, Miss Laura Beth."

Keeping himself between Laura Beth and the dining area, the boy wrangled her into the kitchen and motioned a heavyset teenage girl over. The aroma of garlic and thyme filled the space. "Miss Laura Beth, this is Bonnie Gustrom, the owner of your clothes. Bonnie, Laura Beth Copeland. Bon-bon, I need you to get Miss Laura Beth out the back door."

"What's up?"

"I'll tell you later. Just help."

"All right, Clyde." With a jerk of her head she said, "Come this way."

Clyde went back to the dining room where Madeleine Becker scanned the patrons. He went up to her and engulfed her in a bear hug. "Grandma!"

Her face against the young man's shoulder, Madeleine mumbled, "What the?"

Clyde whispered in her ear, "Miss Laura Beth's goin' out the back door." Louder he said, "Let me get my stuff from the truck to put in your car." Another head motion had the whole gang of boys headed for the door. Bonnie stood in the kitchen door, arms folded across her chest. Clyde threw her a kiss.

Outside, Madeleine hurried to her car and flew around the establishment. Laura Beth jumped in as the car barely slowed and hid on the floor until they were out of sight.

In the parking lot, Clyde ducked behind the truck as the stranger emerged from the restaurant and got into a black Dodge Charger after looking around the parking area as if hoping to see someone.

Penny Ulmer drove up as the Charger disappeared. "Clyde Dixon, you better have something good for me," she said stepping from her car. "Your brother's watching from Heaven." The sheriff slammed the cruiser's door. Clyde emerged from his hiding place.

~

For a woman in her late sixties, Madeleine did not drive like an old lady. She pressed the accelerator and her Buick LeSabre hurtled down the back roads. She glanced in her rearview mirror. "Nobody's back there, honey. You can get up."

Laura Beth collapsed on the seat with her head against the glass. Madeleine eyed her. "I see you found some clothes. Hope that's not your new style."

Laura Beth laughed. "Clyde got them from Bonnie."

"What?" The older woman looked at her friend. "Oh, that boy?"

Laura Beth nodded. "That little group broke all teenage stereotypes."

"Well, I now have a new grandson—Clyde." She patted the younger woman's arm. "Are you okay?"

Laura Beth nodded, shook her head, and burst into tears. Madeleine said, "Tell me everything that happened."

~

"All of you, shut up!" snapped Penny Ulmer. She marched into the café and announced, "Gus is closed for the night. Everybody, pay your bill and go home. I got seven teenage boys that act like they've been drinking. I gotta sort it out."

"What?" gasped the fiftyish proprietor. The sheriff cut him a cold glare, and he said no more. The patrons grumbled as they paid, and Bonnie packed to-go boxes for several. The woman in charge ushered the seven boys back inside.

As the customers moved out, Penny made several phone calls.

Agent Ed Pickering answered, "Not bad news, please?"

"Sorry. It appears you have two dead agents and another body at the place where you were supposedly hiding Laura Beth Copeland. She's taken off on her own."

"What? Another body?"

"You better get over there." She clicked her phone off and dialed another number.

Noise in the background from an arcade almost drowned out Tanner McGill's, "Hello."

"Tanner, Penny. The skuzzy bastard found Laura Beth, killed the two agents and somebody else, and she's taken off apparently with Madeleine Becker. Oh, and she has Cline's gun. She's an armed, pissed-off redhead. Can you say, 'Thelma and Louise on the loose'?"

"What did you say?"

"Look, Pickering is on his way to the so-called safe house, the old extended-stay motel that closed last year for renovations. I'm sure you know the place. I'm getting statements from some boys who might be able to identify the man. I don't think Laura Beth will trust anyone Pickering sends. There's a snake in the midst, and she's smart enough to realize it. She'll trust you. Get her somewhere safe." Without waiting for a response, she closed her phone, called for the department's sketch artist, and then went to talk to a troupe of teenagers.

Penny called over her shoulder, "Gus, feed us. We're gonna be here a while. Put it on the department's tab." She turned to the boys. "Okay, none of this everybody talking at once." She got pencils from the counter and took some of the servers' pads. Tearing off one sheet for each boy from the pad, she handed them the supplies. "Write the description of the man you saw. Then under that write out what happened in your own words." She pointed around the room. "It's just like an ungraded test in school. I want you all at different tables so you can't compare notes. Get busy."

~

Agent Pickering, Agent Sharita Busby, and Agent Diego Marin, who had arrived that morning from Houston, burst into the safe house with weapons drawn. "Oh, shit!" Pickering uttered as the rapidly decaying bodies already sent the pungent odor of death into the room. "When I find out who did this, I swear I'll kill him myself." As the agent in charge, he set about sealing off the crime scene to wait for forensics investigators. "Our boy must think he's the last ninja warrior." He pointed. "Who the hell is that?"

Marin squatted by the third person and searched pockets. He flipped open a wallet. "Virginia driver's license. Says Niall McCormick." He pointed to a sword beneath the body. "Could this be your hitman?"

"Well, who killed him?" snarled Pickering.

With a shrug, Marin stood. "Dissention in the ranks?" He pulled out a badge. "Hmm. Looks like he's one of us."

Pickering muttered, "Oh, shit."

~

Sheriff Ulmer read over each boy's statement. Using a highlighter she pilfered from Bonnie's school bag, she noted the items that were alike. "Boys, was the dude black or white?"

Having grown weary, Clyde grunted, "He was either white or Hispanic. Tanned, but not black."

"Hair?"

"Dark. When we saw the guy on the roadside, he had on a trench coat. It was dark, but he didn't have blond hair. Okay?"

The sheriff narrowed her eyes to slits. "Look, this man has killed a lot of people. You would be nothing more than a nuisance. He wouldn't think twice." She looked down again. "The guy who came in to eat? Same guy?"

"I don't know," replied Clyde. "I couldn't swear it in court."

"Okay. I get it. Are we in agreement that the guy on the road was six feet, give or take an inch; muscular, dark hair, and either white or Hispanic?"

"Yeah."

"What did you say to me?"

"Yes, ma'am. And he had a big nose."

"Yeah, we got that on file already. The guy at the bar? Same size as the man on the road, and same general description? Right?"

"Yes, ma'am. Oh, and I saw a necklace. Maybe a snake. Not sure."

"Metal?"

"Silver or white gold. Oh, and he wears his hair long in a ponytail."

"Okay. Go home, boys. Don't tell anyone what's going on. He might come after you." She turned to the restaurateur. "Gus, you need to come into the twenty-first century. Surveillance cameras would be a big help."

"I don't normally have trouble out here, Penny. I like it quiet."

Clyde stopped to give Bonnie a kiss before he high-tailed it home with his friends.

~

In comfortable, stretch sleep pants and a tank top Madeleine had stopped to buy at the Dollar General, Laura Beth curled her feet under her in the overstuffed chair and sipped the chamomile tea her friend made for her, dropping a pair of flip-flops onto the floor in front of her. Having spoken to her girls, Laura Beth felt a little more relaxed. Two hours after the café ordeal, Madeleine set a plate of Oreos in front of her friend and took one herself. "We have to figure out how to get you somewhere safe," she said around a bite.

"I can't tell you how much I appreciate you. You are a true friend, my foul weather friend. Most people would have run away as fast as they could." Laura Beth ate an Oreo, twisting it apart and eating the middle first.

The doorbell chimed. Both women sat frozen. Laura Beth whispered, "I still have the gun."

"Madeleine, open up. It's Tanner McGill and Doug Blanchard," the detective called loudly through the door.

Laura Beth let out a puff of air that sounded like a tire going flat fast.

12
Need to Know

Madeleine opened the door. The two men entered. In a tone that brooked no argument, McGill said, "Pack, Madeleine. You're going on a trip with Doug."

"What?" snapped the older woman.

Doug Blanchard held up two cruise tickets. "Caribbean cruise for two. Our ship leaves at noon tomorrow from New Orleans. We're in a hotel for tonight."

McGill looked at the petite redhead in pajamas. "Do you have any other clothes here, Laura Beth?"

"Only a couple of outfits Madeleine bought."

"Grab them. We're out of here."

"Where are we going?"

McGill looked around. "Need to know. I'm not even telling Pickering."

"What about your kids?"

"At Grammy's house. All taken care of." He popped his hands together. "Move, women!"

Laura Beth limped toward the guest room. Ten minutes later, she and Tanner headed northeast. Thirty minutes later, Madeleine and Doug headed to New Orleans.

"Where are you taking me?" she asked.

"Need to know."

Laura Beth tilted her head to the side and stared up at the tall blond-haired, blue-eyed man. "I need to know, Tanner. This isn't your car."

"Nope, it's my ex brother-in-law's. My wife's sister's ex-husband. It would be hard to track the name. He has two and let me borrow one."

"Yeah." She nodded with her brow furrowed. "I can see how that trail would be hard to follow. I didn't understand a damned thing you said." She rubbed her face with both hands. "Well, yeah, I did, but I'm pretty smart."

"Yes, you are." He glanced at the woman in the passenger seat. "You look tired."

"I am."

"Sleep."

"Not until I know where we're going."

The detective took a deep breath. "Okay. First, your girls are no longer at their grandparents' house. Ted, the owner of the car, has taken the whole lot deep-sea fishing off the coast of Key West."

Laura Beth sat up straight and glared at the man, her chest tight with anxiety. "You trust this Ted?"

"Yes." He nodded emphatically. "He took a bullet for me. He was my partner. He lost his left arm and now owns his own security company. He's based out of Meridian and works all over the southeast. I made sure your girls are safe."

She settled back into the soft leather of the Lexus Tanner drove. "Thanks. Now, where are we going?"

"Appalachian Mountains. A little place called Possum Holler."

"Let me guess—Ted again?"

"No. My stepfather's sister has a cabin there. They used to disappear there for weeks at a time. She told me to use it anytime I want. Well, this is a good time."

"And how are you paying for this?"

"I'm not. You are." Tanner grinned.

"What? I lost all my credit cards and cash when I spilled my purse."

He dipped his head toward the glove box. "Look in there."

She opened the compartment and pulled out an envelope of money. "Tanner?"

"I requisitioned it from the department. Those are your tax dollars at work. This is now a joint operation with the city, the county, and the Feds."

Laura Beth returned the money to its hiding place. She sighed. "I'm tired, but I can't sleep."

"Why don't you tell me what happened. Describe the person to me."

Laura Beth sat back and related the incidents of the day. "He's an agent, Tanner. How else would he have known where I was, and how else would there not have been a struggle with Cline and Kilpatrick? That third man must have been his partner. Pickering was working on the need-to-know premises, too. They knew those men. They trusted them enough to let them in."

"I think you're right. That's why I haven't told a soul where we're going." He tapped his shirt pocket. "I got a prepaid cell to check in with Pickering from time to time. Mine is on his desk as a paperweight letting him know I took you. That's all the info he gets."

"I need to pee." She pointed at a sign indicating a rest stop ahead.

They took a short break and stretched their legs, used the facilities, and got a snack to continue the drive. Not long after the stop, Laura Beth fell quiet. Tanner glanced toward her. She was asleep. The detective gently moved wisps of hair from her face and sighed.

~

Near dawn, Tanner parked at a Stuckey's and nudged Laura Beth. "Hmmm?" She yawned.

"Do you want some breakfast? I'm starving."

"Sure. Coffee."

The two ordered huge amounts of food and dug in. After the meal they wondered through the store as any tourists might. They bought a couple of t-shirts and sleep pants. Laura Beth found a pair of sneakers and stretch jeans, and she got toiletries.

They loaded the car and left again. "How much longer?" she asked.

"About an hour. There's a small old-time general store where we can get food and supplies. The place is, um, off the grid."

"No electricity?"

"None."

"Running water? Gas?"

"Propane for heating the pumped water and a propane stove."

"Pumped? As in lever?" Her eyes grew round as saucers.

"Well, yeah. It pulls water from a well on the property and stores it in a big cistern. Then you can fill the kitchen sink to wash dishes, a small bathtub for bathing and an old-fashioned toilet. At least it's not an outhouse, but you do have to heat a few pots of water to make hot water."

"Oh, my God," she moaned.

They rolled into a town that had to have had less than a thousand people even including the outskirts. Laura Beth mumbled, "Maybe I can count them on one hand for the census bureau?"

Tanner laughed. He ventured into the small store and bought supplies for a month while Laura Beth waited in the car. She asked when he returned, "Do you think it'll be that long?"

"I don't know. I won't bite you though."

"I'm not afraid of you, Tanner."

"Try not to be afraid at all." He gave her arm a light squeeze. "I'm taking care of you now."

The tires crunched over loose gravel as they rounded a curve and turned down a fairly short drive half hidden by overgrown nandina shrubs. They unloaded the car. Though semi-primitive, the cabin was solid and the surroundings tranquil. Laura Beth stopped on the porch and listened to the call of a whippoorwill and breathed clean air, heavy with the perfume of gardenias and honeysuckle.

They stepped inside. She furrowed her brow. "There's only one bed," she noted looking into the second room of the small lodge.

"I'll take the couch," Tanner said.

"You're too tall to sleep on that couch," she noted looking at the old flowered settee in earth tones. "It's little more than a love seat. I'm almost too tall for it."

The man laughed and held up a roll of material. "Sleeping bag."

"No." She shook her head decisively. "I bet it's pitch dark here too."

"Well, yeah."

"That settles it. I hate the dark. We'll share the bed. Just don't snore."

~

Agent Ed Pickering staggered into the office space he was using at the local police station. He saw the cell phone lying on a handwritten note and groaned. He read the hastily scrawled message:

Have taken Laura Beth. Don't ask where. Need to know. Will call you.

TM

"McGill," Pickering snarled. "You're in over your head. You might get both of you killed."

The agents who had gone with Pickering to the safe house dragged in behind the man. "What's got you scowling even more, Ed?" asked Agent Diego Marin.

Pickering showed him the note. "Is this McGill any good? Or is he just a good-old country boy with a badge?" Marin asked.

"Don't sell him short. He's smart. I know he was a Marine. He did a tour in Afghanistan, bomb disposal. That's why he's so mad at himself about the car bomb. He didn't see signs of it."

"Humph." Marin plopped into one of the two chairs in front of the desk, laid his cowboy hat on Pickering's desk, and crossed his cowboy-booted foot onto his black jeans. "Was he Special Forces?"

"No, not like you."

"So, what if he's your boy?"

"Huh? McGill? No way. No, I hate to say it, but our killer is one of us, as you noted about the McCormick sack of shit." Pickering's brows knitted so tightly they merged into one. "You just came in from Texas, right?"

"Yeah, after Montoya got injured. The boss thought you could use another hand."

"Where have you been for the last few weeks?"

Marin grinned. "Need to know. You don't need to know."

Pickering fingered the phone McGill had left. "You know, I like you just about as much as I like Montoya, right?"

"Feeling's mutual."

"You're arrogant and too damned cocksure. When you fall, you're gonna plummet. And I'm gonna laugh."

"Well, I guess you'd better get to looking for the elusive killer. For the moment you're my boss, so whatcha want me to do?"

"I need to talk to Mrs. Copeland. I bet she can identify the jerk now. Let's find her." Pickering made a shooing motion with his hand. The agent still standing left, and the two remaining men engaged in a Mexican standoff.

A knock on the door jamb got the men's attention. Pickering with a measure of surprise said, "Sheriff, what can I do for you?"

"Not much. But maybe I can help you."

"Have a seat." He indicated the chair next to Marin.

Removing the Stetson with the county sheriff's insignia from her short kinky hair, Penny glared at the agent she was expected to sit next to. "Alone. Need to know."

A low chuckle came from Pickering. "I guess she just put you in your place, Marin. Shoo. Go home, shower and have breakfast. Be back in a couple of hours."

Marin stood and gave Penny a look that would have made most women scream and run away. She stuck out her hand. "Sheriff Penny Ulmer."

Taken by surprise at her assertiveness, Marin shook her hand. "Diego Marin."

The sheriff pursed her lips. "What school?"

"Excuse me?"

"What school of martial arts are you proficient in? I can tell by your hands." She rubbed his hand between both hers, turning it palm up. *Smooth. No stains. No blisters.* "I'm Shotokan and Brazilian jujitsu."

"Oh. Kenkojuku, jujitsu, and nitjitsu."

"Bo, nunchucks, and short blades. You?" She finally let go of the man's hand.

"Name it, sister, but I'm a master of the blade. My katana is personalized." He gave the sheriff a long, lingering once-over. *Damn! That's one hot chick. And she's into martial arts. Yum.*

"Well, I'll just call you 'Highlander.'" Penny's comment shook the agent from his thoughts. "But remember—There can be only one."

Marin scowled and stalked from the room at the dismissive tone. The sheriff closed the door firmly behind the man and leaned against it for a long moment. She cracked it to be sure he had left.

"Piece of shit, son of a bitch!"

"Whoa!" said Pickering. "What's that all about?"

Penny walked toward the desk pointing backward. "That's your man."

"Prove it. We have one dead supposed agent who was apparently proficient with a sword."

The sheriff handed the agent copies of statements from every person at Gus's. She jabbed her well-manicured finger to the highlighted areas. "Get those boys in here without him knowing. I bet they identify him at the very least as the man from the café."

"Okay? What did he do that was illegal?"

"Nothing there, but I just know it. I bet he has the sharpest long blade outside the Orient. That man is a killer, pure and simple. He enjoys it."

"He was Special Forces."

"Even more reason to be concerned."

"I don't like him, Sheriff Ulmer, but I have no proof he was even here before tonight. And I doubt I can discover where he's been. I think he still does covert assignments."

"Then maybe your Perez fellow has connections higher up the chain."

"That's scary."

~

Outside, Diego Marin shivered. "Wow! That is one hot chick, and she's as good as I am." He licked his lips.

He pulled out his cell phone and dialed a number. When the party answered, he said, "McGill's taken her and nobody knows where."

"Find her and you can get rid of that one-horse-town cop too."

Marin heaved a sigh into the phone. "Yeah, yeah." He hung up and dialed another number.

When the connection was made, he pushed several buttons before he screamed into the phone, "Give me a human!" Then he pressed the zero repeatedly until a human picked up.

"Put me through to Secretary Collins."

"Who's calling and what is the nature of your business?"

"Special Agent Diego Marin. National security."

"Hold please."

After several minutes, the person returned to the phone. "I'm sorry sir, but she's gone for the day. Can you tell me what it is you need? I am her executive assistant."

"No! You don't need to know. This is a waste of time." He terminated the call and ran his hands through his hair. He gripped the elastic band holding his ponytail and jerked it loose; his raven hair fell over his shoulders. He dialed another number.

"Mosely," came the answer.

"Collins is out. I'm sure now, Mosely."

"Did you talk to anyone else?"

"I'm not a fool."

"Get the proof."

He snapped the phone shut and was tempted to throw it with all his strength. He took a deep breath. *Go with the flow, Marin. Finish this job and disappear.*

13
Put Your Feet Up

Laura Beth woke to the smell and sizzle of patty sausage. She staggered into the kitchen. "Ow."

"Good morning," said Tanner. "What's wrong?"

"My feet are torn up."

"Sit and put your feet up."

Laura Beth eased into one of the four ladderback chairs, pulling another to use as a footrest. "I ache all over."

"No doubt." Tanner set sausage, scramble eggs, and old-fashioned, buttered-first-and-baked-in-the-oven toast on the table along with fig preserves. He poured two cups of coffee from an old-timey drip coffee pot and pulled milk from the cooler he had packed.

"My, my, the man can cook."

"I'm a single father, remember?"

Tears smarted the new widow's eyes. Tanner looked at the floor. "Sorry. It does get easier to talk about. My only advice is to hold on to the good memories. I'm certain you have many."

Laura Beth brushed the tears from her cheeks. "Yeah, I do." She took a big gulp of coffee. "Thanks for the food and the security. I do feel safer with you."

"That's my goal."

She snagged a piece of toast and a perfectly browned sausage. Taking a bite of bread then meat, she mumbled, "Yum," around the bite. "You really can cook."

~

After breakfast, Tanner forced Laura Beth onto the small sofa. He came to her with a bowl of warm Epsom-salt water. "What are you doing?" she asked.

"Put your feet up here on the table."

"Table?" she said with a wry grin.

The man chuckled. "Crate used for a table. Feet up. I saw how scratched up you are. I'm making sure you don't get an infection. Then, I'm taking you to see the little country doctor they finally got here. I noticed the 'Possum Holler Health Facility' as we drove through."

"How long do you think we'll be here?"

"No clue, but I want to keep you and the baby healthy. Don't argue with me. I'm a lot bigger than you, and I will carry you like a caveman if need be."

"I'd like to see you try." Laura Beth laughed at the thought, the first real laugh she had uttered in a week.

"What would you do? Bite me?"

"I might. I'd do whatever I had to."

"I'm just sorry you're having to do anything." He dried her feet. "I wish I had noticed something amiss with that damned car."

"Not your fault, Tanner."

The detective carried the bowl of water to the sink and dumped it. "You think you could sketch the man again now that you've seen him more closely? And not the guy at the restaurant because there's no proof it was the same man."

"I can try. You know, it was almost dark when he came to the safe house and twilight as I ran. Still, I'll give it a shot."

~

Tanner and Laura Beth drove into the semblance of a town. The small-town doctor, MacKenzie Reardon, looked the woman over. "Any complications with your past pregnancies?"

"No. Why?"

"Well, your blood pressure is elevated."

"I wonder why," she said sarcastically and explained the situation to the doctor.

The man shook his head in disbelief. "Well, if this person tracks you here, he must be a Fed. You won't find Possum Holler on any map. I want you to take it easy. The man waiting outside is a cop, right?"

"Yes."

"Is it all right if I discuss what I'd like for you to do and not to do with him present?"

"Sure."

Dr. Reardon brought Tanner into the room for the discussion. "Mrs. Copeland's BP is up a bit, but under the circumstances, I can understand. Still, I'd like to eliminate as much stress as possible. Might I suggest that you two pretend to be a couple? The Stewarts own that little hunting lodge. I haven't seen any of them in years. If anyone around here asks your names, why not say you're Liz and Tom Stewart? Your secret is safe with me."

The doctor handed Laura Beth a bottle of vitamins from a pantry for his supplies. "I assume you left home without yours."

"Yes. And lots of other necessities."

"Dent's General Store has most things you'll need, but I can get you fresh meat from the slaughterhouse. Is that old rifle still at the cabin?"

"Yeah," said Tanner. "I plan to do a little hunting."

"That's good. And the creek is only about a quarter mile through the woods. Good fishing."

"I saw a rod and reel at the cabin."

"Okay. Mrs. Copeland, I'd like you to come back to see me next week if you're still here. I just want to monitor you. I'm here if you need me. You know that cell phone in your pocket, Detective, is useless around here. No reception. If you need me, get to town. Liz, take it easy. Let Tom take care of you."

She nodded. "Yes, sir."

Tanner took her back to the cabin after a trip to the slaughterhouse with the doctor for pork chops for dinner. As they drove, he joked, "Well, Liz, what do you think of your new husband?"

Laura Beth laughed. "I think my new husband had better not take his role-playing to the extreme, but for the most part, he's dashing and gallant. Now, Tom, do you want me to peel potatoes while you cook pork chops?"

"Nope. I want you to sit back with your feet up."

"You'll get no argument from me."

~

In Sunrise, Mississippi, Agent Luis Montoya entered the house owned by Officer Marge Dixon. He waved his hands in the air. "No bandages."

The officer laughed and her daughter, Deannie, clapped. Marge said, "That doesn't mean you're ready to go back to work though. I still have a week of leisure."

"I thought you'd be ready to ship me back to the hotel."

"And lose my free babysitter?" The woman clucked her tongue and rolled her eyes.

"Why don't you just stay?" asked the little girl, batting big blue eyes fringed in lacy lashes.

Luis laughed. "Little Goldilocks, that would depend a whole lot on what your mother has to say."

"Can he, Mommy? Can he stay?"

Marge's mouth dropped open. "Deannie, Mr. Montoya is not a puppy. He has a job, and he lives in Texas."

"Actually," the man corrected, "I don't technically live anywhere right now. And I'm not certain I want to stay with this job." He shrugged. "Got any openings on the force?"

"Not my department." Marge retreated to the kitchen.

The child took Luis's hand. "Let me see how bad you were burnt."

She led him to the sofa where he sank into the cushions. The little girl turned both hands, over. "They're still pink."

"New skin."

"Do they hurt?"

"Not so much now."

Deannie climbed onto the couch beside their house guest. "Mr. Luis, how old are you?"

"Twenty-seven."

"You're the same age as my mommy. Do you like her?"

"She's a very nice lady."

The little head shook back and forth. "No. I mean do you *like* her?"

The agent looked toward the saloon-style doors that led to the kitchen. The aroma of baking bread tickled his nose. He leaned down and whispered in the child's ear, "Yes."

She nodded with satisfaction. "Okay. Wanna watch cartoons?" She handed him the television remote. He sat back and flipped on the screen, slipped off his boots, and propped his feet on the coffee table. The little girl nestled beside him, and he put his arm around her. Soon *Bugs Bunny* could be heard over the soft snores of both.

After setting a loaf of sourdough bread on the counter, Marge Dixon had listened to the whole exchange. She watched the two carefully. None of the men she had dated seemed ready to be a stepfather. She ran her fingers through her short blonde hair.

You're one of the good guys, Luis. Deannie adores you, and you're good with her. Still, stay? I really don't want to be involved with another cop. But I like you. I really like you.

As if he heard her thoughts, Luis slowly opened his eyes from the cat nap he had been taking. He lowered Deannie onto the sofa to continue sleeping and walked to the kitchen door. "What would you think if I opened my own security company? Maybe bail bondsman and bounty hunter?" he asked, his small, nearly black eyes twinkling.

Almost as tall as the man, Marge met his eyes with mist in hers. "I think I'd like you to stay."

With now steady and healed hands, Luis reached for the woman's face, cradling her head. He pulled her in for a gentle kiss. The kiss deepened, bringing a choked sob to the woman's throat, her fears threatening to overwhelm her. She wrapped her arms around his waist and walked backward, pulling him into her bedroom. With one hand, he pushed the lock on the door and then maneuvered Marge to her bed. They were lost in the moment and each other; their lovemaking gentle and uncertain as if neither had ever had a lover.

Sometime later, he whispered in her ear, "I need to know. Can you fall in love after so short a time?"

"Yes."

"Good, because I love you."

~

Another week passed. Tanner dragged Laura Beth back to the doctor. Her blood pressure was still elevated. A second week and a third went by. At that time the doctor insisted, "I want you doing little or nothing. I don't want you hunting or fishing with Detective McGill. I don't want you cooking or cleaning. Sit back and keep your feet up. You're beginning to retain fluid as well. Are you certain you're not due until September?"

"That's what my obstetrician said."

He measured her abdomen. "This is a big baby."

"I don't do anything when I go into the woods with Tanner but take pictures. How is that stressful? I'll be bored and scared while he's gone."

"Get a different hobby. I mean it, or I'll restrict you to bed rest."

"Maybe if I could talk to my girls, I'd feel better. I'm worried about them."

The doctor tapped his pen against his patient's chart. "Don't move."

Dr. Reardon returned with the cordless phone from the base at the front desk. "Make it fast."

Laura Beth dialed her mother's cell phone. She had a hurried conversation with her mother then spoke to each little girl. Tanner McGill walked in to find his charge on the phone. He snatched it from her and disconnected the call.

"What are you doing? What if he traces that call?"

Big brown eyes blinked back tears. "They're still in Key West. I miss my children."

"So, do I," he snapped. He reared toward the doctor, holding the phone like a club. "How could you let her do that?"

"She knows the girls are all right now. It might help with the blood pressure."

"If *he* doesn't trace us." The detective ran fingers through his hair. "I don't know where else to run, Laura Beth. I've checked in with Pickering twice since we've been here by driving far enough out to get a signal. Nada. They still haven't arrested anyone." He squatted in front of the woman he was beginning to care about and looked up. "Penny thinks she knows who it is, but no proof. I need you to do that drawing so I can fax it to Penny and Dixon. I won't send it to Pickering just in case Penny's right." He rested a hand on her knee. "I know it'll be hard confronting the demon in your mind, but once you do, you can move forward. We've wasted a lot of time because I didn't want to push you too hard."

Laura Beth brushed tears from her cheeks. "I'm sorry about the phone call. I just needed to hear their voices."

He patted her leg and stood. "I understand. I called my kids once."

The doctor cleared his throat. "If you really need to escape and rough it, there's a clubhouse up near the waterfall. I built it with some friends years ago, but it's still standing."

"Thanks. If we need to, we'll go there." Tanner helped Laura Beth down from the exam table. "Are we done today?"

"Yeah," said the doctor. "Remember what I said."

"What did he say?"

"I can't do anything," Laura Beth grumbled. "I'll tell you on the drive back. Does Dent's have a sketch pad and pencils?"

"We'll check before we leave. If not, I'll make a run to Wilmington."

"Next week, same time," said Dr. Reardon. "Then, I'll be in Chicago for a short time. My mentor has asked me to speak to a new class of general surgery doctors."

Both nodded.

14
I Don't Have a Catcher's Mitt

Tanner discovered Royce Dent's daughter was an artist who had left Possum Holler. Because of her, the store owner stocked all manner of art supplies, but he had moved them to the back of the store since his daughter's departure had been under strained circumstances. Dent refused payment for the supplies, and Tanner got a sketch pad and pencils for Laura Beth. Still, she took another two days to begin her sketch.

As Laura Beth drew, she forced her mind not to think about the man at the café. Yet, she knew it was the same man. Sitting alone on the small loveseat, she relived the nightmarish few minutes in the hotel. *It was almost dark. I can't say I saw his eyes. He did have a ponytail, and the eyes looked dark. He was muscular and apparently immune to pain. I kicked him in the gonads. He barely flinched. I don't think his intent was sexual, just downright mean. He was there for one purpose—to kill me.* She sighed. *It almost seems too easy getting away from him as I think back. What was it he said? He didn't want to do anything to me, but he had orders.* She jotted her notes to send with the sketch. Then she began her drawing beneath the words.

She heard a couple of pops and knew Tanner had shot some wild game for supper. The idea of boiled squirrel with rice in the broth, corn bread, and sweet potato fries actually tempted her appetite. The baby bowed into her ribs, and she rubbed the spot until he changed position. Laura Beth sat up and finished the sketch, and then got a couple of sweet potatoes from the bin in the small root cellar to help with the meal.

Tanner came into the cabin a short time later with two skinned and dressed squirrels. "You read my mind," Laura Beth said, holding up the potatoes, peeled and sliced into fries.

"You were working," Tanner scolded.

She set the bowl down. "That was easier than this." She retrieved the sketch and handed it to the cop.

He scowled deeply, eyes hooded to the point of almost being closed. "I've seen him somewhere." He laid the picture back on the table. "I'll fax it tomorrow. Dr. Reardon has a fax machine."

Laura Beth grunted.

"Are you okay?" Tanner asked.

"Yeah." She rubbed her abdomen. "Someone's in a bad position." She pushed herself off the sofa.

Tanner arched his eyebrow.

"Stop scowling," she said. "I have to pee, and that means walking. I just love that old pull-the-chain toilet. At least it's not an outhouse even if you do have to fill that cistern for water frequently." She grinned. "Better you than me."

The detective laughed, laid the game in the sink, and took the potatoes from the stubborn redhead.

~

After supper, the two refugees sat on the plank porch, Laura Beth with sketch pad in hand. "It's really beautiful here," she commented. "Although summer, the mountains offer a gentle coolness." She inhaled the fresh scent of pine mingled with honeysuckle. Crickets, cicadas, and owls presented a soothing symphony.

Tanner watched her hand travel delicately across the canvas. "What are you drawing?" he asked.

"You."

"I'm flattered."

Laura Beth caught her side. "Oh, somebody is really misbehaving."

"Have you considered a name?"

"Yeah. I think my maiden name plus Bruce."

"Excellent. What is that maiden name?"

"Riker. Riker Bruce Copeland." She sighed and bit her lip.

Tanner moved a little closer and gently laid a hand on her shoulder. "He'll be a good man, just like his dad. Tell me about you and Bruce."

"He was a junior. I was a freshman going through rush at Ole Miss, pledging the sister sorority to his fraternity…"

They talked until the moon hung high in the sky.

~

The next day, Tanner drove to town and faxed the sketch to Penny Ulmer. He drove far enough toward the small town of Wilmington to get a signal on his prepaid phone. Pulling onto the shoulder of the road, he dialed Ed Pickering. When an unfamiliar voice answered, Tanner terminated the call instantly.

"More Feds?" he asked the air. "Not talking to somebody I don't know."

The policeman did a U-turn and headed back to their safe little hamlet. He stopped at the slaughterhouse and got a small pork loin. Remembering Laura Beth had mentioned the day being her birthday, he went to Dent's General Store to purchase a strawberry cake mix and frosting. While there, he bought a set of rhinestone barrettes and a bottle of White Oleander cologne.

The proprietor smiled at the purchase. Tanner shrugged. "It's Liz's birthday."

"That's nice. Are you baking the cake?"

"I am."

"It must be love."

Tanner chuckled and left with his purchase.

The door to the cabin creaked as it opened. Laura Beth dozed on the miniature sofa. Tanner laughed softly. He leaned over the back of the couch and held a small gift bag in front of the lady's face.

"Wake up, Sleeping Beauty. Happy birthday."

Laura Beth started from a dream. "Oh!" She sat up, rubbing her eyes. "How sweet." She took the bag.

Tanner turned to the kitchen and cake preparation. He hand-whisked the batter and set two round pans in the oven.

"What do you think?" She had put the barrettes in her hair, pulling the sides back from her face. Laura Beth turned her head from side to side.

"Beautiful."

She opened the cologne and sprayed a bit. "Old Spice!" she blurted.

"What?"

"He smelled of Old Spice. And sweat. And something a little bitter and sweet mixed."

Tanner sat beside her. "His cologne is a big memory. Scent is important."

Auburn hair bobbed across her shoulders as she nodded. "Gasoline. Maybe on his boots."

The detective spiked an eyebrow. "Maybe he recently pumped gas and spilled a bit? I'll have to let Pickering know to check gas stations close to the safe house."

Brown eyes lit up as the aroma of baking filled the air. "Strawberry cake?"

"Huh-hum."

"My favorite."

~

A couple of days passed, and Laura Beth visited the doctor before he left for Chicago. Dr. Reardon smirked. "BP is a little better. Keep taking it easy. I'll be gone two weeks. I'm saying again—You won't make September. I think your due date is off."

"How off?"

"When was your last period?"

"That's the problem. I was on Seasonique."

"Well, without a sonogram, I'm guessing more like the end of July."

"No wonder I feel so miserable."

The doctor laughed. "Just hang in there. I'll only be gone two weeks."

~

For a third time, Tanner drove out of town to try to contact Pickering. He left his charge still sleeping with a breakfast of oatmeal, fresh blueberries, toast, and bacon covered on the stove.

Finally, Pickering himself answered the phone. "About damned time!" Tanner exclaimed.

"McGill, where are you?"

"Safe. Did Penny get the fax?"

"Yeah. That sketch worries me."

"You know him?"

"Think so, but it's still iffy."

"Well, she had another breakthrough. She said he wore Old Spice and she smelled gasoline. Maybe he pumped gas nearby. Cameras or clerks might peg him."

"I'm on it."

Tanner drove into the larger town of Wilmington to get supplies unavailable at Dent's store.

~

Half awake, Laura Beth staggered to the kitchen. "Tanner!"
A note on the table read:

Gone to call Pickering. Breakfast on the stove.
I'll splurge for Hamburger Helper tonight.

She laughed and caught her side. She grimaced with the cramp and waddled to the tiny cubicle called the bathroom. Her underclothes felt damp.

Laura Beth scowled at how wet her panties were but dressed comfortably in lounge pants and a large t-shirt. She returned to the kitchen and ate the breakfast Tanner had left for her.

Standing from the table, a contraction seized her, and she doubled over.

"No, no, no," she stammered. "Too soon even for Dr. Reardon's prediction."

Before she could straighten, her water broke. "Shit! Where are the cops when you need them?"

Laura Beth gripped the walls to get back to the bed.

~

The proprietor of the general store teased the tall cop again about being in love as he purchased items for dinner, having bought ground round in the larger city. Tanner laughed aloud as he walked toward the car. "Could be," he said under his breath. "Could easily be."

He climbed behind the steering wheel and started up. Driving down the dusty dirt road, large raindrops began to pelt his windshield. He cranked up the radio and sang along at the top of his lungs with Keith Urban and "Days Go By."

Back at the cabin, Tanner grabbed the brown paper sack of groceries and made a mad dash for the cover of the porch as the clouds unleashed like a broken dam. He shook his hair like a dog. It was getting longer than he normally wore it and stuck out in all directions.

He opened the door to eerie silence and total darkness. He lit the Coleman lantern on the table by the door. Straining his ears, he heard groaning in the bedroom. "Laura Beth?"

"Tanner!" The woman's voice sounded thin and frantic.

He set the groceries on the table, lit another lantern, and flew to the bedroom.

"Help!" Laura Beth screamed.

"What the?"

"This baby is coming."

"I don't have a catcher's mitt."

"Tanner, help! No time for jokes!"

The cop inside Tanner McGill took over. He lit the three other oil lamps in the house and checked the woman he was trying to protect. "Oh, Jesus! Help me, Lord."

Tanner raced to the little bathroom and returned with several towels. "Push!" he commanded.

Fifteen minutes later, Tanner clamped the umbilical cord with a twist tie from a loaf of bread and used his hunting knife to cut the cord. Laura Beth heard crying that sounded like a kitten mewling. "How is he?" she panted.

"Small, but he looks good."

"How small?"

Tanner held the baby out in front of him on both hands. "I'd guess close to five pounds. Nice size for a preemie."

The mother held out her arms. "Give me."

"When you're done." He used a clean towel and wrapped the baby snugly, laying him in an open drawer of the old cedar chifferobe in the room, and then finished taking care of Laura

Beth. Once his charge was redressed in clean clothes and in a clean bed, he handed the baby to his mother. "Here you go. Riker Bruce Copeland, meet your momma, one amazing lady."

Laura Beth cuddled the newborn close. Tanner whispered, "Rest. I've got to zip back to town. We need at least diapers and feminine supplies. Are you nursing or do I get formula?"

"Nursing. Thanks. I'm so glad you got back."

As Tanner went to kiss Laura Beth's head, she looked up. Their lips met. Tanner finished the gentle kiss and left to get baby needs. "Are you nuts?" he muttered to himself as he dashed to the car.

Laura Beth's heart raced. She touched her fingers to her lips. "Too soon," she murmured. "Way too soon." She kissed the fuzzy head of Bruce's son.

15
The Long and Winding Road

Tanner barely caught Royce Dent before he closed his small store for the evening. "Mr. Dent!" he called breathlessly racing from the car in pouring rain. "I need diapers and feminine hygiene products."

"What?" asked the owner of the store.

"Laura Beth…"

"Who?" the store owner interrupted.

Tanner felt like kicking himself. "Liz had the baby a little early."

The merchant looked skeptical. "I won't say a word. You're not hillbillies, so I figure you're hiding from someone."

"I'm a cop and someone's trying to kill her. But she did have the baby, a boy."

The businessman opened the door. "Come on. Get what you need."

Tanner bought the items he needed and once again drove until he had a signal. He phoned the FBI. When Pickering answered, voices argued in the background.

"I'll make it quick," said Tanner. "She had the baby early. This has taken a toll on her. Catch the bastard." He terminated the call without giving the agent a chance to reply.

~

In Sunrise, Mississippi, Agent Ed Pickering left his office in a huff. "Marin, you fit the description. So did Montoya, and I did, too, to a degree. Get over it. What kind of cologne do you wear?"

"Old Spice. Why?"

Pickering frowned and waved a hand as if to say, "Never mind," and the lead agent left to visit the sheriff, forgetting his cell phone in the process.

Agent Marin discreetly picked up the phone and dialed the number that had just called Pickering.

Tanner answered on the first ring. "Not talking with folks around, and I won't have a signal once I top the next hill."

"Listen, please…"

Tanner hung up.

"Damn it! I give up." Marin transferred the number to his own cell. *No, you don't, and you know it. You never quit.*

As he laid Pickering's phone back on the desk, the senior agent came back in. "Forgot my phone. What are you still doing in my office?"

"Just lollygagging."

"Well, get out."

"Yes, sir."

For the next several days, Marin dialed the number and always received the message that the number was out of area.

The agent Googled a map of total dead zones in the U.S. He ruled out any west of the Mississippi River and above the Mason-Dixon Line. Most were too far away for McGill to have reached before his first call to Pickering.

Then, he paid a visit to the sheriff's office. Marin had been told McGill had faxed some sort of sketch to Penny Ulmer, but as far as he knew, only Sheriff Ulmer, Pickering, and Officer Dixon had seen it.

Marin paid attention to every detail if Penny Ulmer was involved. His mind raced with possibilities. *That bitch had best not tell me I have to take out Pretty Penny. It won't happen. My best alternative would be to get rid of her, but how? I'm not even a hundred percent certain of her identity! I hate feeling trapped.*

Mosely needs to get busy confirming my theory. Got to go see Pretty Penny without her seeing me. I'd like to see lots more of Pretty Penny.

With all the suits and officers going in and out of the building and the fact he had been there a few times, no one paid him any attention. Watching for an opportunity was tedious though. All office space occupied one end of the building while the county detention center sat on the opposite side of a long hallway. A person had to be admitted to the lockup area. At last, Ulmer went to the ladies' room. Marin took his chance.

He slid into the sheriff's office through a barely-cracked door. He took a brief moment to watch the woman walk. *What an ass! I'd like to wrap my hands around that. I'm crazy. I have to get this done and get out of the country.* He went inside the office.

It was meticulously neat. He attacked the stack of files in the dead center of the desk, expecting the professional woman he had met to have the most important material closest to her workspace.

Two folders down, he found what he sought. The file contained one faxed sheet of paper. He stared at the sketch and read the notes.

"Well shit! Stupid bitch!" he muttered. "You must want to die. If I can find you…" A sly grin crossed his face. Using the Sharpie from Ulmer's desk, he wrote the fax number that appeared in small print onto his hand.

The agent cracked the door to see Ulmer speaking with Dixon. He slipped through the door and out the building entrance at a brisk pace. *Pretty Penny would take my head off.*

Back in his hotel room, Marin pulled up a reverse look-up on whitepages.com. "Dr. MacKenzie Reardon, M.D., Possum Holler, West Virginia," he mumbled. He searched for a map of

West Virginia and studied it intently for a long time. "Where the hell is Possum Holler, West Virginia?"

~

The next morning, Marin entered the police station where the FBI had temporary office space. Officer Marge Dixon snapped pictures left and right.   Luis Montoya stood with her and laughed.

"What's up?" asked Marin of his fellow agent.

"Ooh," exclaimed Dixon. "Look." She stuck out her hand to show an engagement ring.

Montoya explained, "This is my last case. I'm leaving the Bureau, marrying this lovely lady, and setting up a private investigating and bail bondsman and bounty hunter business here."

"Well, congrats." Marin's smile looked more like a sneer.

"Oh, oh," said Dixon. "Stand together for a photo."

Marin grunted but stood next to Montoya. Dixon snapped a shot. Marin moved on, mumbling, "I hate pictures."

"That man is one sour puss." Dixon stood next to Montoya. "Well, I'm still saying, 'Yes.'"

He put an arm around her. "I hope so, but you got his picture."

"Yeah. Now, I need to print." They exchanged a quick kiss and went their separate ways. Dixon headed to the CVS Pharmacy to print a picture. An hour later, she gave a copy to Penny Ulmer who faxed it to Dr. Reardon who was in Chicago rather than his office.

~

Puffing out his cheeks and rubbing bloodshot eyes, Marin pushed back from the laptop on the table in his hotel room. "Does the place exist?" he said aloud and messaged his temples. He researched Possum Holler, West Virginia, until he found one news snippet about a cave-in at a coal mine thirty years earlier. He grinned and tightened a fist around the pen he held. "Found you. Good move, McGill. Now, can I get you to listen? Sorry, but Little Momma needs to disappear." *It might mean my head,* ran through his mind. He laid the pen down and leaned back in his chair, gripping his own hair with both hands. He let out a long breath. *Time to move.*

~

Just after dark, dressed completely in black, Marin left his hotel room in a black Dodge Charger with dark tinted windows. On the passenger seat, lay an antique super-sharp katana, its intricately carved ivory hilt and tsuba with entwining serpents peeking out of the leather sheath. He lowered the weapon to the floorboard and tucked it under the seat. *I hope I don't have to use you, Kireina Meiyo.*

He got on the interstate and opened the engine full-throttle. The specter-like car zoomed along, nearly silent for fifteen hours. He stopped only a couple of times for the restroom and food.

His adrenaline pumping, Marin drove up and down the country road that was supposed to lead to Possum Holler. "Damn it! This place has to exist. I found the mines."

It was well after dark the next evening. Marin slammed his brakes, screeching to a stop with the smell of burnt rubber and a thin trail of whitish smoke.

He got out of the Charger and stared down a dirt road that would be difficult to traverse with two cars passing. "This is little more than a goat path," he muttered. *Reminds me of the Andes in some ways.*

The man eased the black car down the long, winding, rutted, road, finally coming into a small smattering of houses. The dash clock read 9:00 P.M., but he rationalized it might be ten in the Eastern Time Zone. No lights shone in the town. He continued through the municipality and turned down each drive or road.

At last he spied what he was looking for—a Mississippi license plate. The cabin near where the Lexus was parked was pitch black. His foot touched the cold metal under his seat. A grimace crossed his face. *Please listen to me this time.*

~

"Laura Beth, wake up," Tanner said with a gentle shake.

"I just fed Riker," she mumbled.

"Get dressed fast. We have to move." He kept his voice low.

"Why?"

"A car just stopped outside. Nobody knows we're here but Royce Dent and Mac Reardon. Dent wouldn't come out here this late, and the doc is still in Chicago."

Laura Beth dressed in the dark, her hands trembling. She felt cold steel being slipped into the waist band of the jeans she put on. "What?" she began.

"You said you shoot straight. You might have to. Mine is on my side. I have a knapsack with a few necessities." He handed her the baby.

Just as the couple slipped out the back door, the front door flew open.

"Run! No time for the car!" Tanner led the way into the woods on a starless night.

"Where are we going?"

"That clubhouse Reardon mentioned."

~

Inside the cabin, a possible assassin flew into a rage, throwing all manner of items as his quarry once again eluded him. He lit two of the Coleman lanterns. One he tossed into the center of the house. He took the other, broke a window on the borrowed Lexus, and threw the flaming oil lamp into it. He started through the thicket in search of his prey, thoughts in a flurry. *What do I do? Damn! I need to bring her in. Maybe I can make folks believe she died in the fire. Madre María, Santa Madre de Dios, dame sabiduría. Ayúdame a resolver esto. Quiero que esta sea mi última misión, al igual que Luis.* He made a quick sign of the cross.

The resounding boom as the propane cylinder on the stove exploded and the orange glow drew Tanner and Laura Beth's attention.

"Shit!" exclaimed the cop. "Let's move it, Sugar."

Riker began to whine. "Keep him quiet," Tanner said. He grabbed Laura Beth's hand, and they raced through the woods.

16

Safe Harbor

"Keep moving," Tanner encouraged his charge.

"I don't hear his footsteps," Laura Beth wheezed.

"Our advantage. I know these woods and hills now. He doesn't. Still, I'm betting he's military. He'll adapt. I hope it starts raining." Tanner stopped short as they clambered up a steep rise.

"I'm hurting, Tanner. How much farther?" Laura Beth caught her breath in gasps behind him. "How can the tree frogs sing so jauntily?" she grumbled.

"They're praying for rain, just like me. Good frogs." The man panted, "There's the clubhouse, but do you see that?" He pointed toward the cascade. "Is it a little cave behind the falls?"

"Looks like it," she eked out.

"If the light's not just right, you couldn't see it. Come on, Sugar. That's where we're going."

After a little more climbing and navigating slick rocks, they dropped behind the waterfall into a small cave stocked with a straw mattress, a foam pillow, and a number of plastic containers.

"Somebody knows about this place," said Tanner. He picked up a notebook that lay on top of one of the plastic containers. "Alain Richter." Squinting in the dim light, he read the name on the cover. "Met him. Maybe he'll shoot the bastard for trespassing. He's a bit scary himself."

The baby began to whimper and wiggle. Laura Beth collapsed onto the makeshift bed and fed her son. Tanner stood sentinel near the curtain of water.

"Sh," he breathed. "He's here."

The man chasing them climbed above the waterfall as the sun tried to peek through saturated clouds. The pursuer slid back down the slope just beside the cavern as the clouds dropped their load. Though a bit wavy through the curtain of water and dim dawn, Tanner could see the man in all black with the sword slung across his back.

Tanner gave Laura Beth the come-hither finger. She stood beside him and watched as the man headed back to the clubhouse. He stopped to notice the little shack was wedged closed from the outside. He turned a full three-sixty. Tanner put Laura Beth behind him in case the man saw the cave. The cop pulled his gun from its holster.

The figure below them shouted, "I need to find you, bitch! You're gonna lose your head. McGill's too! It'll be a miracle if your baby survives. Come on, lady! Get a clue." He took a breath. *Come on. Show yourself. Maybe I can fake your death. Photoshop a picture or something. Maybe I can get McGill to listen.* "You could save us all some trouble. Come out, come out wherever you are," he yelled over the gush of rain and rush of the cascade.

Tanner whispered, "He doesn't know you had the baby. Pickering must have kept it quiet."

After a bit more taunting, the man let loose with a string of profanities and obscenities, many in Spanish, before he loped back through the woods. Wicked lightning cut jagged paths through the clouds. The rain poured harder.

"Thank God," Tanner muttered. "Not even an Indian scout could follow tracks with this kind of rain." He steered Laura Beth back to the straw bed where they both sank in exhaustion. "Did you recognize him?"

She nodded. "The man in the café."

Tanner stretched out on the pine straw covered with blankets. "Let's rest. I'll figure something out." He pointed. "If you're thirsty, cup some of the water from the falls in your hands. It's pretty clean."

"I'm okay."

Holding baby Riker to her chest, Laura Beth snuggled into Tanner's outstretched arm with her head on his chest. He let his arm envelop her. They slept. The low roar of the cataract lulled them into peaceful slumber.

~

The black Charger stopped in the cluster of buildings which made up the corporate limits of Possum Holler. Very few people were about on the rainy morning. The driver got out and walked to the place that seemed busiest, Dent's General Store.

A withered old woman exited the store as the tall man with a bulbous nose entered. He tipped his Stetson. "Ma'am." The old lady nodded and paused to listen to what the stranger said to the owner of the store.

Diego Marin pulled his badge from inside his black trench coat pocket. "Agent Diego Marin," he said, showing the badge to several people in the store. He then pulled out two photographs, one of Tanner McGill and one of Laura Beth Copeland. "I'm looking for these two fugitives. I'm certain you good people wouldn't harbor them."

A couple of patrons shook their heads negatively. Royce Dent cut his eyes toward the old lady in warning before he said, "I've never seen the woman. The man bought some groceries."

Sensing an antiquated morality, "She's in the family way," said Marin. "A Dr. Reardon might have seen her."

The old woman hobbled back, leaning on her cane. "I'm Miriam Newton. I'm on the city council. My great-great-grandson is in Chicago." She looked at the pictures. "Ain't seen 'em. If they stopped to see a doctor, I'm sure Mac seen 'em. He's a doctor, after all. What they do?"

"They're wanted for murder." *Mine if I don't get to her soon.*

"Thank you for the warning. I'll load my shotgun."

A balding man ran in. "The Stewart cabin is ablaze even in this rain. Did you hear the blowup?"

"Thought it was thunder," said the old lady.

Dent asked, "Any chance of it spreading to the trees?"

"Don't think so," answered the messenger. "But that fire was set. Ain't no way them propane tanks blew by accident."

Marin said, "Does anybody live there, Mister?"

"Jones. Gator Jones. I seen smoke, but the Stewarts are outsiders. Always kept to theirselves when they come in. Who are you?"

"A G-man," interjected the old lady.

Marin dipped his head in agreement. "FBI." *Among other things.*

The man called Gator scowled. "You might not wanna stay around here, mister."

"I'm looking for two fugitives."

"Well, if they were in the Stewart place, they long gone."

Marin sighed. "If you think I'd waste my time on some backwoods moonshiners…"

"Mr. FBI," the old lady barked with authority. "You best be gittin'!"

Marin stared at the old matriarch who glared back with equal intensity. The agent thought *the old woman doesn't need to fetch a shotgun. She probably has a pistol in the pocket of the cardigan she has on.* He asked another question anyway. "I went all the way to the top of that waterfall. There's a valley. Any way down there?"

"Straight down the mountain," said Gator. "Me and some friends built a clubhouse up there years ago. I figure the road cuts around about ten miles past the heavy forest."

"Where does it lead?"

"A city called Wilmington."

A loud explosion got all their attention. Gator looked out. "Another propane cylinder. Maybe one on the porch. Hey, mister, I could swear I just seen two figures high-tailin' up the road out here."

"Where?" demanded Marin.

Gator pointed. "Yonder way. Kinda hidden in the trees."

Marin jumped into the Charger and went in pursuit.

Miriam Newton turned to Royce Dent as all the patrons, but Gator Jones, left. "Whatcha hidin', Royce Dent?"

The store owner related what Tanner McGill had told him.

~

Late in the afternoon, Gator Jones and two other men, both tall, one blond and one with ponytailed, light-brown hair and a long shaggy beard, approached the clubhouse. "They ain't in the house," said Gator, noting the door was still wedged shut.

"You think they know about it?" asked the blond.

"Yeah, Tipper, Mac mighta told 'em about it. I bet he knows the whole story and cain't say nothin'. That hypocrite oath. "

"Hippocratic," muttered the scraggly one.

"Well, they're not here," Tipper said.

The bearded man looked toward the falls. "Great observation of the obvious," he said. The three men left.

Tanner watched from behind the curtain of water.

"Who is it?" asked Laura Beth.

"One of them is Alain Richter. I don't know the other two. I met Richter while hunting one day." Tanner looked around. "He knows we're here."

"Will he tell?"

"I don't think so."

A short time later, Alain Richter slipped behind the waterfall. Tanner pulled his nine-millimeter. Alain held up his hands. "Relax. I ain't armed. I'm here to help."

The bearded hillbilly took in the situation. "Little lady, you look like you fixin' to fall down. Let's get you to Grandma Newton. Then we'll figure out what to do."

Still not quite sure she could trust anyone but Tanner, Laura Beth held Riker close to her heart.

Alain smiled at her with teeth that needed dental work. "I got two. I ain't gonna let nothin' happen to you or that little one. I only ask that you never tell about my hideaway." He held a hand out to shake toward Tanner. "I'm Alain Richter. I met you huntin' one day, but you said your name was Tom."

The cop shook hands with the man. "Tanner McGill. Detective Sergeant Tanner McGill, Sunrise, Mississippi Police Department."

Alain said, "A fella claimin' to be FBI come into town. He said y'all are wanted for murder. I think it more likely it's him."

Laura Beth nodded. The hillbilly who stood inch for inch with Tanner placed a hand on the woman's back. "Let's go."

~

An hour later, Alain knocked on Miriam Newton's door. The old woman answered with shotgun in hand. "Oh, it's you." She lowered the gun. "What's wrong?"

"I got 'em, Grandma."

"Git 'em in here!"

"He ain't been back?"

"No."

Alain returned to his Ford truck and hustled Tanner, Laura Beth, and the baby inside.

"Lordy mercy!" exclaimed the old lady. "Babies, y'all look wore out. Sit. First, I'll feed y'all. Then, we'll come up with a plan. You, too, Alain. Sit down."

After introductions, the old grandmother served a feast of broiled pork chops, mashed potatoes with gravy made from the pork drippings, butterbeans, cat-head biscuits, and sliced tomatoes and cucumbers. The former midwife examined the baby and the mother after the meal. She grunted, "You done good, Detective McGill. They healthy."

"And alive," Tanner intoned softly.

"Yep," said the old woman. "Now what to do?"

"Where else is left to hide?" asked Laura Beth.

"Right under his nose," said Tanner. "We need to get back to Sunrise." He handed Alain the prepaid cell phone. "Can you use this tomorrow evening, so he thinks we're still on the lam?"

Alain took the electronic device. "Does it work just like a real phone?"

Tanner showed the man how to use the cell phone. Alain nodded. "I got ya covered."

"Me too," said Grandma Newton. "I'll get you to the bus station in Bluefield, Virginia."

"How are we supposed to take a bus?" asked Tanner. "He incinerated most of my cash in the glove box of the car." He reached into his back pocket. "I only kept a couple hundred on me."

Grandma Newton waved off the question. "I got enough to buy y'all tickets. He'll think you'll go to Wilmington. But I'm atakin' you to Virginie!"

"Maybe I should do that, Grandma," said Alain. "He might be watchin' you. He don't know me."

She nodded. "Might be better. Babies, y'all bathe and find some clothes in that old cedar chest. They won't be fancy, but they clean. You'll find some little jumpers for the baby, too. I always gave one to the baby I delivered." She smiled an almost toothless grin.

Forty-five minutes later looking like real hillbillies in jeans and flannel shirts, Laura Beth and Tanner got ready to leave. Grandma Newton placed baby Riker in a big straw basket with a few baby items beside him and some sandwiches wrapped in plastic inside a brown bag near the baby's feet. She handed Tanner a wad of money and pointed at him. "Don't argue."

"Thank you."

Alain said, "Okay, when we go out, I'll call y'all Tipper and Sunny 'cause Tipper's tall and blond and Sunny, the school principal, is a short redhead. It's dark with only a sliver of moon, so if he's watchin', maybe it'll fool him. If it don't, you can shoot 'im, Tanner."

"Thanks, Alain. Grandma, thank everybody in Possum Holler."

"I will. Now y'all git on the road."

The Ford left Possum Holler without incident. At the bus station in Bluefield, Tanner bought another prepaid phone and tickets to the bus station in Jackson. He called Madeleine Becker who left her house immediately to go to the Mississippi capital to wait.

Alain waved the couple off. Laura Beth collapsed in the seat. Tanner squeezed her hand. "You can definitely identify him now. It'll be over soon."

"I hope so." The baby began to whimper. Laura Beth threw a small blanket over her shoulder, opened her shirt, and nursed her son. Tanner put his head back and napped.

With the sunrise, Alain called Agent Pickering and dropped the word West Virginia on voicemail.

As Royce Dent opened his store for the day the next morning, a black Charger stopped in front of Grandma Newton's house. Diego Marin knocked resoundingly.

The door opened. Miriam Newton stood with her shotgun in the man's chest. "Boy, I done told you to git. Them folks ain't here. Don't bring yo city troubles to our town." She raised the gun and fired over his head. "Git!"

A number of townsfolk turned out at the sound of a shotgun in town, including a tall, lanky man that immediately jogged the length of Main Street to the old woman's house.

"Are you okay, Grandma?"

"Jest fine, Preacher Tomlin. This here big-city lawman thinks we hidin' murderers."

"Leo Tomlin," he extended a hand.

Marin shook it and glowered. The preacher smiled. "I suggest you leave. There are no murderers in our midst, but Grandma Newton will shoot you for trespassing, and hillbilly justice will make sure your body's never found."

Marin's jaw dropped. "I'm out of here." He left and headed back to Sunrise, worried about how to eliminate the threat he had been ordered to get rid of. He sighed. *This assignment is out of hand. Mosely! You need to call me.*

Well after dark, Madeleine Becker drove through her gated entrance with two adults hiding in her back seat. "Safe harbor, my friends."

Tanner and Laura Beth sat up. "Now to get Dixon and Penny," said Tanner. "Pickering's got a snake in his midst."

Assertively, Madeleine said, "Not tonight, Tanner McGill. Tonight, you sleep. You can charm a snake tomorrow."

"I'm too tired to argue, Madeleine."

Near midnight, Marin slipped into his hotel room to an unwanted surprise. "Where have you been?" demanded Ed Pickering.

"Following a lead to a dead end." *Almost literally.*

Pickering stood and his cell rang. He answered fast. An unfamiliar voice said, "Play along. Tanner and Laura Beth shoulda reached safety by now. Just ask aloud so anyone can hear, 'Where the hell is Possum Holler?' They ain't here no more. I'm hanging up."

Pickering hollered, "Where the hell is Possum Holler, and where are you now?" He closed his phone. "Damn it. He won't trust me."

17
Snake in the Grass

Gus's Gas and Goulash was open for an invitation-only breakfast. Gus actually served a hearty meal—pancakes, sausage, scrambled eggs and cheese grits—to over a half dozen young men and two law enforcement officers, as well as his daughter and himself.

Once again, Sheriff Penny Ulmer seated seven teenage boys at separate tables. She asked Gus and Bonnie to sit at opposite ends of the lunch counter. She placed multiple sketches and written descriptions in front of Clyde Dixon. "Clyde, you're a better artist than anyone we pay," the sheriff stated. "First, read these descriptions and give me an artistic rendering. Then, look at these other sketches and see how close yours is to them."

"Are you gonna pay me?"

Ulmer glared at the boy. He held up his hands in mock surrender. "Okay, okay. I know. After college with a degree."

Marge Dixon addressed the rest of the young men. "Fellows, you have a stack of photos in front of you. I want you to circle men you recognize with the black Sharpie. If you recognize the man you saw on the road the night y'all helped Laura Beth Copeland, circle him in red." She took a deep breath. "I'm gonna tell y'all my new fiancé is in some of these pictures. I swear to God if he's circled in red, I'll shoot out both his kneecaps before I haul his ass off to jail."

The boys stifled sniggers because they knew the woman was serious. The driver of the truck the night the group rescued Laura Beth raised his hand.

"Question, Rowell?"

"Circle anyone we know?"

"You can forget women. We know we're looking for a man."

"So, circle Detective McGill and the late Dr. Copeland?"

Marge ran her hand through her short blonde hair, closed her eyes and shook her head. "I think we can safely eliminate the late doctor. But McGill? Yeah, go ahead, but if he's in red, he's dead. After you go through the pictures, write up again what happened on the road that night."

She turned to Gus and Bonnie. "I need you two to write up what occurred in here that night and describe the stranger to the best of your recollection. Y'all look through the pictures too."

After a short time, Rod Rowell raised his hand again. "What now?" barked Dixon.

"Well, it was real dark that night. I can't say for sure about the man on the road, but the man that came in here is definitely in one of the photos."

A rumble among the boys started. "Whoa! Stop the chatter," Marge said. "You all see the man that came in Gus's?"

Nods and affirmative comment's ensued.

Officer Dixon asked, "You too, Gus, Bonnie?"

They nodded.

"Do you want us to circle him in red?" asked Rowell.

The two law officers looked at each other. The sheriff nodded. "Yes," Dixon said with authority.

"Sheriff?" Clyde called.

"Yes?"

"How's this?" he slid a sketch across his booth.

Ulmer looked at it and a half-smile crept of her face. "Snake in the grass."

Marge looked over the sheriff's shoulder and handed her the photo each boy had circled. "Marin."

Ulmer nodded. "If he'd just got here from Texas, what was he doing in here?"

"Dinner? That's what a good lawyer would argue. It is sort of on the way to town if he followed road signs." Dixon played the devil's advocate well.

The sheriff waved the faxed sketch Laura Beth had drawn. "This one's Marin, too."

Marge nodded. "Very close. Close enough to question him. Pickering will be pissed."

"Tell me something new," the sheriff sniped. "He's always a grouch."

Ulmer's cell vibrated as the women talked. "I don't know the number," she said looking at the display screen. The vibration stopped.

Dixon's phone blared a loud, "Star-spangled Banner."

The boys hooted with laughter. The police officer glowered at them. "Same number," she said.

"Answer," said Ulmer.

"Officer Dixon," Marge said into the phone.

"I'm glad one of you is willing to answer an unknown number," said Tanner McGill.

"Where are you?"

"Nope. Not saying."

"Boss," Marge argued, "you know I'm a good cop."

"Not the issue. Pickering has a snake."

"Yeah. Penny and I think we know who it is."

"Really? How?"

"Good police work, and he thinks we're a bunch of bozos and he's superior to us." Then she laughed. "But the way he stares at Penny's ass, I think he wants to jump her bones."

The sheriff popped the other policewoman on the arm as if they were high school girls. The boys snickered and mumbled comments.

McGill said, "Well, I don't know a name, but the bastard somehow found us in a nothing town...no, village...wait, hamlet...maybe settlement would be more appropriate...in West Virginia. The place is mostly off the grid and not on the map. He tracked us somehow, so he's good. But here's the news. Laura Beth recognized him. She said it was definitely the man that came into Gus's the night we took off."

"Shit!" Dixon nodded vigorously to Ulmer. "Marin."

"Is that his name?" asked McGill.

"Yeah, Boss. Agent Diego Marin."

"Well, I suggest you charm the snake away from his blade or there could be a blood bath."

"So? Snag him at the office?"

"Sounds like a plan to me."

"How are y'all?"

"Fine. She had the baby early. I delivered him."

"She's a tough one. I like her, Boss."

Barely above a whisper, McGill replied, "So do I."

"Ooh!" Marge bubbled. "Montoya and I are engaged."

"That was fast."

"It clicked."

"Think if I share a pizza with 'you know who' it'll click?"

"Could be."

"Yeah. Maybe. Anyway, get the info to Penny."

"She's standing right beside me."

"Glad to hear it." The phone clicked in Dixon's ear.

"What?" demanded the sheriff.

"Mrs. Copeland identified the man who came after her and McGill at their hiding place as the man who came into Gus's."

"Gotcha!" Ulmer turned to the group of boys and the Gustroms. "Not a word to anyone about this morning. You wouldn't want Sir Ninja Snake to come after your heads. Y'all did the right thing. Now, take off."

The young men and Bonnie Gustrom didn't need to be told twice. The sheriff put a hand on Clyde's shoulder as he started out. "You get that art degree with a criminal justice minor or vice versa and you have a job." Ulmer jutted her chin toward the door. "Time for school. I'll call the principal in case you're a few minutes late."

Clyde stopped beside Marge for a moment. He spoke quietly. "So, you're over Claude, huh?"

"I'll always love your brother, but I think he'd want me to have a life."

"Yeah. Is this Montoya a good guy?"

"Would I settle for less?"

Clyde shook his head. Marge put an arm around her dead husband's younger brother. "Listen," she said. "You're still my little brother. Deannie's still your niece. You need to visit. Get to know Luis. Give him a chance."

"Okay. How about we all go bowling Saturday? I'll bring Bonnie."

"Sounds like a plan." She kissed his cheek. Clyde joined his friends. Gus got ready to open for business.

Penny dialed the school and then Tanner McGill.

"Yes, Penny?"

"Bring her. She'll have to make a statement to Pickering for us to nab the son of a bitch. Safety in numbers. We'll meet you there." She did not give McGill time to respond.

18
Jimmy Durante You Ain't

Laura Beth shook from head to foot when McGill told her she had to go to Pickering's office. Whether from rage or fear, Tanner couldn't be sure. "Look, Sugar..." he began.

"Stop calling me Sugar!" she snapped.

"Sorry." He released a deflating sigh.

Running a hairbrush through her long auburn locks, she turned from the mirror over the dresser in the bedroom she had used the night before at Madeleine Becker's house. "I have been scared shitless, run off the road, watched my husband die, fought off a man twice my weight, run barefoot through a briar patch, hidden in a pile of rotting leaves"—She ticked off each event on her fingers—"Had bugs crawl into my private parts..."

Tanner had to bite his lip not to laugh on that one.

"Damn it, Tanner! It's not funny. He might have a mega-schnozzle, but Jimmy Durante he ain't."

The cop rolled his hand over and over to indicate for her to continue. "Please finish your enumeration, oh, census-taker."

"Screw you!" She turned back to the dresser and placed her hands on it, not sure if she could stand without the support. Her legs felt like cooked spaghetti.

"Whoa!" He put his hands on her shoulders and massaged the tense muscles of her neck.

A half sob left Laura Beth's throat. "Then I ran off with a gallant knight to a one-horse town, lived off the grid with limited amenities, delivered a baby at home way too early, fled through the woods, hid in a cave, had a kind caveman offer assistance, came to my good friend's home, and didn't sleep a wink last night

141

because you slept on the couch. I've grown accustom to your little rumbling snore. I feel safe hearing it."

She turned around and laid her cheek against Tanner's chest. "If you call me 'Sugar,' am I supposed to call you 'Cream'?"

"Maybe 'Cream Puff' when it comes to you."

~

Impatient fingers drummed on his desk as Agent Pickering waited on hold, one of his pet peeves. Finally, a voice said, "Steve Journey here."

"About damned time. I hate being on hold. Ed Pickering here."

"Ah, yes, what can I do for you?"

"Well, that Detective Reynolds in Eau Boueuse, Louisiana, thinks you're the cat's meow, the kingpin, the cream of the crop. He reamed me out so badly when I talked to him, anything positive about the Bureau must be good, so when he dropped your name more than once, I figured it was time to call. His first response once he finished his tirade was, 'Where are Lawrence Dantzler, Patrick Swift and Steve Journey on this one? You need Journey. He's the best.'"

"You need a profiler?"

"I'm not sure. Are you up on the Perez case?"

"I've scanned it. How can I help?"

"Tell me what I should look for."

"You're not going to want to hear it."

Pickering slammed his fist on the desk. "Just give me your opinion."

"Okay." Journey took a breath. "It's an inside job, one of our own, in a way. It's at least someone who has lots of inside information. Your guy is very intelligent, a master martial artist, military background, probably a lone wolf, but very dedicated to his country. This guy is not working on his own. Someone is giving him orders. Has he made any serious slip-ups or said anything weird when you've talked to him? And I know you have."

"He did say Perez didn't hire him."

"He's giving you clues, hoping you'll figure it out and stop whoever is making him do something he's not comfortable with."

"Okay. He killed a stripper."

"Ah. Self-preservation. I bet she tried to extort something from him. With that mistake hanging over his head, he knows his days are numbered. Whoever's in charge won't care if he's caught and/or killed. The head person is probably hoping for the latter. That way he can't talk. I'd put money on a burn notice on him right now."

A number of rapid taps with a flat palm indicated Pickering was thinking. "Journey, let me throw a name at you. Tell me what you think."

"Shoot."

"Diego Marin."

Pickering heard Journey clicking on a keyboard. "I haven't met Marin," Journey said, "so I'm reading his bio. He's pretty new to the Bureau. Career military and no evidence of retirement. Special Forces. Army Intel. Hmmm. He has no family, an orphan that was raised in a Catholic children's home. Decorated hero, but there are gaps in his history that would indicate covert ops. He's a master of the martial arts, especially katana. IQ off the charts. He definitely fits your boy's profile. And he's there now, right?"

"Yeah."

"But he seems to have a code of honor. I see one refusal to obey orders, but then that's where his blanks start. Think long and hard before you bring him in."

"Thanks."

"Anytime." The call ended.

Pickering sipped the coffee in front of him and grimaced. "Ugh! Cold." He ran both hands across his head and yawned. The stocky man got up and went to refresh his coffee, mumbling, "I've been here for months and still don't have my own coffee pot."

As Pickering entered the break room, Penny Ulmer and Marge Dixon came in the front door. Looking around quickly, Dixon said, "I don't see him." The two women marched to Pickering's office.

"Well, where's Pickering," grumbled Ulmer.

"I'm right here, Sheriff," Pickering said with a scowl on his face and holding a steaming cup of coffee. "To what do I owe this dubious pleasure?"

The agent sat at his desk and indicated two cast-off dining chairs with a flick of his thumb. The women sat.

Immediately, Ulmer flipped open the file she held. "I told you when I met him, Marin was your man."

"Based on a handshake and martial arts training. I need more proof than that, Sheriff."

"Try this on for a fit—He found McGill and Mrs. Copeland in a little place called Possum Holler. She recognized the man who came after them as the man in the café." She spread the pictures of Marin that every young man, and both Gus and Bonnie Gustrom had circled. "And the boys, every single one, identified him. So did Gus and Bonnie." She jammed her finger on one photo. "Marin is the man at Gus's."

"Well, shit!" Pickering reached for the file, knocking his coffee over. "Damn it! I'm already pissed, and I haven't had my coffee quota."

Ulmer snatched her evidence from the path of flowing liquid.

Pickering reached in his desk drawer and withdrew an assortment of fast food napkins, plunging the mass into the spilled coffee.

"Want me to get you some more?" asked Dixon.

"No!" He threw the wet glob of napkins into the waste can with enough force to rock the metal container. "When did you gals discover this for a certainty?"

"This morning," said Dixon.

"And we came straight here," finished the sheriff.

"Marin hasn't come in yet," Pickering said. "When I talked to him, he said he'd been following a lead. He's always been a rogue bull, but the asshole has taken orders from somewhere really high up in the past. He's 'on loan' right now."

"You think he's with some other organization spying on you," observed Ulmer. "You think he's following orders. Who that high up is dirty?"

"I refuse to say until I have evidence to go over her head. Besides that, he's only been identified as the man at Gus's, not anywhere else." The agent puffed out his already chubby cheeks. "Where's McGill?"

"On his way here," answered Penny.

"Here," confirmed McGill from the doorway with Laura Beth and the baby held in a carrier shielded in front of him.

The two female law enforcement officers immediately began to gush over the baby. McGill rolled his eyes and Pickering slammed a hand on his desk. He bellowed, "I'm sure he's precious, but let's get busy keeping his mother alive."

Laura Beth entered the office warily and took the chair Ulmer vacated. Dixon took the baby carrier to the side of the room and set it on the floor. Pickering said, "Sheriff, you got any more pictures without circles?"

"Yeah."

With a wave of his hand, the agent said, "Give the lot to Mrs. Copeland."

Laura Beth took several photos. Pickering asked, "Do you recognize anyone?"

She nodded. "This is Agent Montoya with him." She tapped the picture of Montoya with Marin. "That's the man that came to West Virginia. He was at Gus's."

"You're certain?"

"Yes. Sorry. Is he one of yours?"

"He's an agent of some kind. Is he the man that came to the safe house?"

Laura Beth sighed. "I can't say for certain."

Pickering looked around at the officials. "We need to figure out how to take him down without killing him. He's lethal with that sword and his bare hands." He rubbed the back of his neck. "And I do think he's taking orders from up the chain. If he'd wanted you dead, you'd be dead."

McGill still stood with his back against the door. He asked, "You think someone with the Bureau is on Perez's payroll?"

"Higher up than the Bureau," said Ulmer.

"Shit!" exclaimed the local detective.

"You think this man's just been following orders?" asked Laura Beth, her voice shrill. "He murdered my husband and a stripper. How were they a threat to anyone?"

Pickering sighed. "I understand your feelings. I'm just afraid Marin is a pawn, too. But, damn it! Sometimes you have to question orders."

"Okay," said McGill. "How long has Marin been with the Bureau?"

"Not long. He was Special Forces and I know he did some covert stuff with CIA clearance." The older man bumped his hand on the desk. "It was my understanding he'd retired from the military and came on with the Bureau right about the time Perez went to trial, but I just found out he's not retired."

"Too coincidental," said Ulmer.

"Yeah." Pickering rubbed his head. "Now I have to take their killer down." He eyed Dixon. "I'm sorry I ever thought Luis was involved."

The woman waved it off, her engagement ring sparkling. "Don't worry. I threatened to shoot out his kneecaps if the boys identified him, but I knew he was one of the good guys."

The sheriff cleared her throat. "Look. Maybe, Marin was under orders and didn't question them, but that man is a cold-blooded snake in the grass. He enjoys killing." Pickering started to speak. Ulmer shook her head. "Don't blame the military. I spent thirteen years in the army, two tours in Iraq. I'm not a mass murderer."

Pickering said, "But you weren't trained to be an assassin."

"No. Look, you can defang a poisonous snake, but the snake handler will just find another snake."

"Yeah?" Pickering knitted his brows together.

"So, we need him alive. We need him to tell us who calls the shots. It's one thing to take out the enemy, but some official has targeted innocents and our own."

A knock on the door made conversation cease. Pickering indicated McGill to get Laura Beth to a corner and for the sheriff and Dixon to position themselves on either side of the door.

"Pickering?" Marin called.

"Yeah! Come on in."

Marin opened the door. Penny Ulmer flung the man to the center of the room. The two female law enforcement officers barred the door and drew their weapons.

"Surprise," Laura Beth said with surprising calm. With her foot, she pushed the carrier the baby was in beneath a table.

"You are a venomous snake caught in a trap. Time to pay for your crimes."

Pickering held out an open palm toward a chair. "Take a seat, Marin. Let's figure something out."

19
Straight-Shootin' Son of a Gun

Marin looked around him and chuckled. "Tell me something, Little Momma. When did you figure it out?"

"Me?" Laura Beth touched her chest.

He nodded. Laura Beth said, "If you'd just kept driving, I'd never have been able to identify you."

"It wasn't my call. Just saying there was a black Escalade had you in deep shit. I was told to make sure you didn't talk."

"By whom?" Pickering asked.

"I'm not stupid. I'm not saying another word."

"Marin, you're a fool. Even you must realize there are times to question orders. Whoever is yanking your chain, will choke the life out of you." Pickering tried to reason with him.

Marin laughed outright. "I'd like to see her try."

"Her?" asked Penny Ulmer.

Marin gave the entire group a tight-lipped sneer. "Not even for you, Pretty Penny."

Eyes wide, nostrils flared, Ulmer inhaled sharply and took one step toward Marin.

"Yes," Marin continued in a voice to make Barry White proud, "I'd love to spar with you under different circumstances."

Pickering slapped the top of his desk. "So, where do we go from here, my man?"

Marin shrugged. "I know where I'm not going." He sat down.

Tanner McGill's hand slid to his gun, and he blocked the door. Dixon and Ulmer made a protective wall in front of Laura Beth.

Marin laughed out loud and held up an index finger. He put his hand to his side holster.

Tanner's sidearm came out. "Don't think about it."

Marin took his gun out carefully and placed it on Pickering's desk. "Argentina sounds good to me."

"You have to be kidding!" Laura Beth squealed from behind her human shield.

"Lady, I don't kid."

"You're a cold-blooded killer. What did Bruce do to deserve to die? What about that stripper? Your colleagues?"

Marin shook his head and leaned back in the chair, raising its two front legs off the floor. He put both hands on top of his coal black hair, and then stretched both arms over his head.

With lightning speed, cat-like agility, and the fluidity of running water, Marin bent backward, flipping the chair over. In the same motion, he somersaulted and brought his right foot across Tanner's hand, knocking the detective's weapon into the air. A split second later, the heel of Marin's left cowboy boot connected with Tanner's face, hitting with enough force to crack the detective's cheek bone and knock him to the floor.

Almost simultaneously, Marin flung the overturned chair into the two women blocking Laura Beth. He caught Tanner's gun before it hit the floor, grabbed the other padded chair from in front of Pickering's desk and fired through the seat, which muffled the sound. The bullet struck Pickering's upper left chest just below his collarbone. Marin burst out the door and fled the premises.

"Oh, hell no!" screamed Laura Beth. Before any official could react, the petite redhead snatched Marin's gun from Pickering's desk and flew after the escapee.

Marin headed for his black Charger, unlocking the door via the remote on the key fob. As he whipped the door open, he felt searing pain in his left buttock which quickly spread to the right. He dropped to a knee.

"I'm a straight-shootin' son of a gun, you sorry piece of shit!" Laura Beth shrieked. "When I aim, I don't miss."

~

Penny recovered quickly. She grabbed Dixon's shoulder. "Take care of Pickering."

Penny followed closely behind Laura Beth. Holding his broken jaw, Tanner lumbered beside the sheriff.

"Are you okay?" she asked.

"Hurts like hell," he replied through clenched teeth. "She'll kill him, Penny. I can't believe we're trying to keep the bastard alive."

~

"It's a flesh wound," Pickering moaned as Marge Dixon put pressure on his injury.

"Shut up, you stubborn goat." Marge summoned an ambulance and paramedics.

"It didn't hit a vital organ," Pickering argued. "He didn't want me dead, or I'd be dead. I'm telling you right now that something is really up with him."

Paramedics came through the back entrance of the police station. Dixon waved them through the door. "Get him to the hospital."

"Go!" said Pickering. "Keep that crazy little woman from doing something stupid."

Riker began to cry. Dixon picked up the baby. "I've got my ammo right here."

~

Marin pulled himself onto the driver's seat. He felt red-hot pain in his left shoulder and saw stuffing from the passenger seat poof out. A second bullet had gone clean through his shoulder. He slumped over the seat. He felt steel against the base of his skull.

"Sugar!" Tanner called. "Stop."

"No!" Auburn hair whipped back and forth as she shook her head. "Drop your gun," Laura Beth ordered Marin.

Marin let the gun fall between the seats of the car.

Roll over," she commanded. "Look at me while I put a slug in your brain."

The man slowly turned over and stared into the barrel of his own gun. "You won't kill me. You're not a murderer, but damn! I like you. You're almost as wonderful as Pretty Penny."

"What?"

Marin groaned.

"Laura Beth, take a step back. You aren't safe that close to a trained assassin," Tanner said.

She backed up a couple of steps. "You didn't answer my questions earlier," she said.

"What were they again?"

"Why Bruce?"

"Oh, yeah. Sorry. *Nobody* was supposed to be in the car. Bruce always left at seven. The car was on a timer to go off a half hour later. I'm glad you weren't in that car. I like you."

"I hate you," she bit out.

"I figured." Marin's voice rang of sadness.

"Why those two nice agents? And that other man?"

"Other man, I did. He killed Kilpatrick and Cline."

"Bullshit! Not good enough." Laura Beth fired into the seat beside the man's head.

"I wanted to talk to them—tell them the whole story. Cline pulled his gun. McCormick didn't give me a chance to speak, just sliced their heads off, and then I took his."

I did hear voices. They seemed calm at first. Laura Beth's thoughts began to blur.

"And the stripper?" she demanded bringing herself back to the present.

"Wasn't me. McCormick."

Laura Beth shot the metal of the car, two inches below Marin's crotch. "Try again."

"Ugh." He tried to shrug. "She could identify him. Self-preservation. Pretty Penny's more my type though. I only set the car on fire to cover his ass until I could find out who he worked for."

"You're not mine," growled Penny Ulmer, gun drawn and standing two feet behind Laura Beth. "I don't like snakes."

"You would've enjoyed this one."

Laura Beth aimed directly at his penis. "Shut up. Do you pray to any god? Do it quick."

"Laura Beth, put the gun down," said Penny. "We need him alive."

"Sugar," said Tanner, "we have to go up the ladder. We need him."

"I'm not talking, McGill," Marin said.

McGill snorted. "You will, or should I let Laura Beth use the remaining eleven bullets?"

"Little Momma won't kill me." Marin sounded cocksure.

Ulmer snarled, "Laura Beth, shoot him somewhere else that won't kill him."

Laura Beth glanced over her shoulder. Penny and Tanner were now within two steps of her. Other officers stood at a distance. Tears glistened on Laura Beth's cheeks.

Marge Dixon appeared behind Penny and Tanner. "Laura Beth," she said softly, "your son needs you. You have two little girls who need you. If you kill him, you'll go to jail too. Back away now and let Tanner cuff him. He knows if you'd meant to kill him, you could have done it easily."

The woman with the gun trained on the man she thought was a killer looked back at Marin. "You are despicable. I wouldn't believe a damned thing you say. You don't deserve to breathe the same air as Bruce Copeland's children."

Marin nodded. "You're right. So, end it."

"How did you get to be so loathsome?" Laura Beth asked.

"Uncle Sam trained me, ma'am."

"Shoot him already!" snarled Tanner. "How dare you? I held the body of my best friend as his life oozed from him when he stepped on a mine. A piece of the metal pierced my left kidney. Military doctors were able to save it, but I got an honorable discharge and a purple heart. Don't you dare tear my country down! Uncle Sam never took away your choice not to kill innocent people. Whoever is giving you orders is the enemy. Tell us who it is. Stop this madness. Or we can all walk away and never see Laura Beth shoot you."

Voice tinged with remorse, Marin said, "You wouldn't do that either, McGill. *Semper Fi.*"

Tanner took a deep breath. He laid his hand gently on Laura Beth's extended arm. "Sugar."

"Cream," she said in a voice choked by tears.

"Cream Puff. Give me the gun."

Laura Beth lowered her arm and handed Tanner the weapon.

Penny slapped cuffs on Marin. He groaned. "Easy, Pretty Penny. Little Momma shot me in the ass."

"You'll always remember you poked the wrong pig," Laura Beth snarled.

The police officers who had stood back rushed to assist the sheriff. Dixon stepped forward and handed Riker to his mother. Tanner put an arm around Laura Beth. She touched his already swollen cheek. "Get that looked after. I'll be fine."

"It's over, Sugar."

"Almost." She tiptoed to kiss his cheek. He turned his head. Their lips met. She finished the soft kiss, smiled, and walked away with Dixon.

20
Laying the Past to Rest

A hand bearing a chocolate milkshake poked through the door of Tanner McGill's hospital room. "Is it mocha?" he asked, his voice light despite the pain he felt.

"No, sorry, just dark chocolate." Laura Beth came in. "How are you?

"Fine. They're keeping me overnight just as a precaution. I don't have a concussion; just a cracked cheekbone. I can't eat steak for at least three weeks, not that I can afford it." He took the shake and slurped a big swallow. "But I can have these in abundance. Thanks."

Laura Beth pulled the chair in the room closer to the bed and sat. "I checked on Pickering. No lasting damage, but I bet he gets a medal. He'll be in here a few days."

"Where's Marin?"

She snorted a laugh. "Next door. He's cuffed and shackled to the bed; a guard inside and outside."

"Is he talking?"

"Nope."

"He will." Tanner drank more of his shake. "He wants to save his own hide. Right now, he thinks being quiet is the answer, but he'll change his mind."

"Do you really think someone high in government is the real villain here?"

He nodded. "Yeah. Unfortunately."

Auburn hair spread across the back of the chair as Laura Beth put her head back. "I get to sleep in my own bed tonight. It'll be strange."

"When will the girls be home?"

"Tomorrow." She drummed her fingers on the arm of the chair. "Day after tomorrow, they're releasing Bruce's remains."

They locked eyes. She smiled faintly. "I kind of need you to help me here. Just in case I fall apart, I need you to pick me up."

"What can I do to help?"

"Just be around."

"Not a problem, Sugar."

"Cream." She squeezed the man's hand and stood.

As she walked out the door, Tanner whispered, "Cream Puff." *She is so under my skin.* He sighed. *And in my heart.*

~

The sanctuary of Sunrise United Methodist Church was packed. Family, friends, former patients filled the pews to finally lay Dr. Bruce Copeland to rest. The minister talked about how Bruce had followed the Great Physician and offered healing and comfort to those suffering.

Several patients spoke about the man who had gone far above what was required.

Madeleine Becker stood. "Bruce Copeland gave much more than medical care. He gave himself. Several times during my chemo, Dr. Copeland himself took me home because I had no family nearby. He used to joke that his wife would think he was having an affair. Then I had the privilege of meeting Laura Beth. Bruce loved her and his children so much. Sharing them with a sick old lady gave me the desire to keep fighting. I'll miss him, but he has left a lasting legacy of love."

The older woman, also a widow, made eye contact with Laura Beth. The young widow smiled at her. Madeleine sat down.

On the other side of the sanctuary, Tanner McGill, with his two children beside him, rose. His face several shades of blue and purple, he cleared his throat. "I hate speaking before a large group. I lost my wife to breast cancer nearly four years ago. Bruce Copeland was her doctor, but there was very little he could do for Tina. He arranged for her to spend her final days at home. She passed in the presence of all those who loved her, among them—her doctor."

Tanner looked toward Laura Beth. "The last two days of Tina's life, Bruce never left her side. He never left *my* side."

Laura Beth thought about the times her husband had spent with his patients. She had to admit she had on occasion resented some days that he didn't come home. Hearing the testimony of these people she had come to cherish quickened the tears to flow. *Selfish, selfish, selfish.*

She stood on shaky legs and walked to the closed casket with a photo of Bruce on top of it. She traced the outline of his face with her index finger. "I always knew Bruce was extraordinary. At times I was jealous of the time he gave to all of you."

She turned to face the crowd. "I felt cheated, but now all of us have been cheated. I understand now that Bruce's gift of healing went much deeper than medicine. He comforted the spirit. Now"—She waved her hand palm up in an arc—"I'm glad he touched you.

"Although I might not know all of you by name, we all share the honor of having known Bruce Copeland. Whether he was your doctor, your colleague, your friend, your loved one, he has left an indelible mark on all of us. We are better for having known him."

She turned back to the coffin and ran her hand across the mahogany. There were few flowers by request. Money that would have been spent for floral arrangements had been donated to the American Cancer Society. Laura Beth touched her fingers to her lips then to the photo of her husband. "I love you. You're in the care of the Great Physician. You have no need. All of us will leave here and endeavor to live a life worthy of being saved by a physician like you, and like the One you served."

She turned back to the people in attendance. "Go now and live. Live life to its fullest. Remember that if you want to offer a token in Bruce's memory, make a donation in his name to cancer research."

~

A private interment for family only in the church cemetery was followed by a gathering at the Copeland home. Madeleine Becker, Penny Ulmer, and Marge Dixon directed the mourners as they entered.

Laura Beth, the children, Bruce's parents and family and Laura Beth's family arrived forty-five minutes after the others.

Laura Beth made her way among the mourners with a word for each. She came to Ed Pickering, his arm in a sling. "Thank you for coming, Agent Pickering."

"I wish…"

She shook her head. "Don't."

"Are you okay?"

"I will be. How about you?" She pointed at his arm.

"I'll live."

"Will you be leaving soon?"

"We have a few loose ends."

"Of course." She laid her hand on his. "Excuse me."

She made her way to Marge Dixon and Luis Montoya. She smiled at them. "You see. Even the two of you have been blessed by knowing Bruce. You found each other."

Montoya started, "I'm so sorry we…"

"Not your fault," she cut him off.

Luis nodded. Marge squeezed Laura Beth's hand. She, too, had lost her spouse in an act of violence. A silent understanding passed between the two women.

Penny Ulmer approached Laura Beth. They hugged. "Thanks," said Laura Beth.

"I wish I could have done more."

"You've been a great help."

The mourning widow noticed seven teenage men and one girl. She approached the group. "Y'all are awesome. I owe you my life."

Clyde Dixon spoke for the group. "We'd do it again."

She patted the boy's arm and moved on to Madeleine. The older woman hugged her. "I'm tired, Madeleine," Laura Beth whispered.

"Disappear."

"You think I'll be missed?" She looked over the gathered throng. Grandparents had the two girls. The baby had been placed in his crib upon arrival. Laura Beth kissed Madeleine's cheek and weaved her way out and down the hall to the nursery.

She opened the door quietly. Riker was stirring. She picked him up and sat in the rocking chair to nurse him. He had already gained over a pound. When he finished eating, she cradled him in her arms and rocked.

"How I wish you could have known your daddy." Tears splashed onto Riker's face and he kicked with discontent. Laura Beth backhanded the tears from her cheeks.

A tap at the door startled her. The door opened and Tanner came in. "I thought you might be here. Do you want a sandwich or anything?"

"Can you sneak me some Coke without giving away my hiding place?"

He held up a red and white can. "I thought you might want this. Trade?"

Laura Beth handed the baby to Tanner and took the soft drink can.

"Hey, little man," Tanner said in a soft coo. "I've kind of missed you."

The baby's face scrunched up and a little rumble indicated a diaper change. Laura Beth laughed. The man hooded his eyes. "I've got this," said Tanner and took care of the baby.

He used a sterile wipe on his own hands when the change was finished. He picked Riker up and rocked him back and forth in his arms a few minutes, humming softly.

Laura Beth watched with interest. After a short time, the baby slept again. Tanner placed him in the crib and covered him with a blanket.

Laura Beth sighed. Tanner knelt beside the chair. "You need to go to bed," he said.

"Too many people."

"I'll take care of it."

~

Within half an hour all guests were gone. Laura Beth's parents headed back to the Coast. Bruce's parents stayed a little longer to put Stacey and Tonya to bed. Tanner walked out with them and locked the door.

"Detective McGill, will you check on them?" asked Mrs. Copeland.

"Yes, ma'am."

"Then we leave them in good hands," said Mr. Copeland. They made their way home.

Tanner joined his son and daughter in his car. He paused before cranking.

"Dad?" said Corbin. "Do you like her?"

"Yeah," the man admitted.

"You gonna ask her out?" asked Roslyn.

"It's too soon," said Corbin, punching his sister's arm.

"Ouch!"

Tanner said, "Maybe once the past is laid to rest."

"Fine," said his son with a grin.

"Let's go home."

~

As Tanner and his children watched TV, the phone rang. "I have to get it?" asked Tanner when neither child made an effort.

"It won't be for us," Corbin said. "Bet you gotta go to work."

"I hope not. That would mean a crime has been committed." Tanner grabbed the phone on the fifth ring. "Hello."

"I can't sleep."

"Laura Beth? What's wrong, Sugar?"

"I need some Cream."

"What?"

"I can't fall asleep. I'm scared to close my eyes."

Tanner looked at his children. "Do you have a place my brats can crash?"

"Guest room and sleeper sofa."

Corbin turned off the TV and grinned at his father.

"We're on our way," assured Tanner.

~

Laura Beth waited in the doorway as the McGills arrived. The kids brought in overnight bags. The woman smiled at them. "I never officially met you. I'm Laura Beth."

Tanner said, "Corbin and Roslyn."

They entered the house. Laura Beth said, "I already made up the sofa."

"I'll take it," said Corbin.

"Okay," responded Laura Beth. "It's late. This way to the only furnished guest room. We've only been in this house about a year."

Tanner gave his son a kiss on the head and he and Roslyn followed Laura Beth down the hallway. Roslyn sat on the bed in the guest room. "Where will you sleep, Dad?"

Tanner looked at Laura Beth. She turned beet red. "Roslyn," she stammered. "I kind of need your dad with me. We've been on the run so long, I'm scared without him."

"I bet," said the little girl. "That man was real scary."

"Yes, he was. I'll be okay soon, but I need my protector."

"I understand, Miss Laura Beth. Dad's big and strong and scares the monsters away."

Laura Beth's brown eyes stared into Tanner's blue ones. "Yes, he does."

Tanner kissed his daughter's forehead, and she slipped under the covers.

Outside the guest room, he said, "Lead the way."

They stepped two doors down. "What are you sleeping in?" Laura Beth wore sleep pants and a tank top.

"What I have on, ma'am."

She laughed. "You've slept in boxers beside me before."

"But there were no children around."

"Good point. Still, jeans won't be comfortable."

"I'll be fine. If I'm needed again overnight, I'll invest in a pair of sleep pants."

"Okay."

Laura Beth lay on her side of the bed. Tanner lay beside her. She tentatively put her head on the man's chest. He smiled in the dark and cradled her in his arm. "Night, Sugar."

"Night, Cream." A small giggle escaped her throat.

"Cream Puff."

21

Vows and Oaths

Back to a quasi-normal routine, Tanner walked into his office to see Marge laying a piece of paper on his desk.

"What's that?" he asked, a tightening in his chest as he thought Dixon might be resigning. *She's an excellent assistant. I don't want to lose her.*

"Request for leave, Boss. Now that you're back, Luis and I are moving forward with wedding plans."

"So, you aren't quitting?"

"Nope."

"Good. You know I had no choice about the suspension, right?"

"Yeah, Boss. It's cool. You can't get rid of me that easy, but Luis *is* leaving the Bureau and forming his own investigations and security business, but I'm here. He'll also act as a bail bondsman and bounty hunter." She smiled broadly. "My husband might need an official hand from time to time."

McGill laughed. "Am I invited? When?"

"Of course, you are. Labor Day weekend. Saturday. Not big. Penny's my maid of honor." She cracked up. "Think Ninja Man can get a pass? He has the hots for Penny, calls her Pretty Penny. She's creeped out." She laughed harder. "I'll tell you a secret. I think she likes him too. That's what really has her spooked."

"Really? Did I hear you right?" Tanner shook his head as if to dislodge something. "God! Can you imagine the sparring? Let's hope his pass is a one-way ticket to Leavenworth."

"I doubt they'd send him the same place Perez is incarcerated."

Tanner finally sat in his own leather chair and breathed a relieved sigh. He indicated for his assistant to sit. She slid into the chair on the opposite side of the desk.

Tanner asked. "Has Marin said a word?"

"No. He vowed silence and said he'd like to keep his own head."

"So? He thinks whoever is calling the shots *will* send someone after him." Tanner rubbed his chin. "Good bait."

The detective turned on his computer. "Marge, when I first saw Marin's sketch, I recognized him. I have research to do. I'll figure it out." He waved her out. "Go plan a wedding, but keep your cell on in case I need you." He rubbed his still-bruised cheek. "By then, I can eat. Have lots of food at your reception."

~

McGill stopped by the hospital. He wanted to talk to Marin. He was surprised by how tight and thorough the security was around the prisoner. Pickering had provided the lawmen serving as guards a list. Even if his name was on the list, Tanner had to show identification, and he was searched. The outside-the-door guard demanded that the detective leave his weapon with him.

Tanner cocked an eyebrow. The guard shrugged. "Agent Pickering's orders. He's concerned a listed person might kill the jerk and/or, and I quote, 'Marin's smart enough and sneaky enough to get the weapon, and then you'd all be dead. I swear if he escapes, I will kill every last one of you myself.' Agent Pickering was serious. Maybe not death, but I'd be in deep shit."

Tanner took off his side holster, being careful to wrap his gun in the strapping. The guard opened a lock box with a combination. With reluctance, the detective placed his weapon in the box. The guard closed the box, spun the dial and opened the door to Marin's room.

The inside guard looked up from the baseball game he was watching. Tanner looked back and forth between the two guards. "His job is cushier." He flicked his thumb toward the inside guard.

"There are three teams of us, twelve-hour shifts," outside man explained. "Every six days, we're off three. To take a piss, whoever's outside has to come in here. Inside steps out. No breaks. Hospital meals served to us by arrangement with Pickering. Yum." Sarcasm dripped on the last word. "We alternate inside-outside days. Three days, morning; switch to evening for three days. Off three days. Repeat."

"I'm making new friends," muttered Marin as he lay face down with his face in an open doughnut-shaped pillow. He could only stare at the floor. Both hands lay beside his head. They were connected to more than one I.V. and long chains on cuffs. "I can identify folks by shoes." He laughed a cold, bitter chuckle. "Little Momma shot me in the ass. I'm having a little trouble with that one since it's become infected. Thanks for asking, McGill."

"I'm not close enough for you to have seen my shoes."

"Recognized your voice. You don't have that classic redneck, taffy-mouthed accent. Cultured southern gent—that's you." He moved his left hand to his side. "You know, I didn't want to kill Little Momma, didn't even try, but after this, I swear I'll take pleasure in cutting off the bitch's head."

McGill stomped to the bed and pressed his hand into the bandage that showed through the split in the hospital gown Marin wore.

The patient bellowed in pain as pus and blood oozed through the gauze. He frantically pushed a button on a morphine pump on one of the I.V.s. "Damn you to Hell, McGill!"

Tanner leaned closer to Marin's ear. "You listen to me. If you so much as look at Laura Beth again, you will beg for death

before I finish with you. As God is my witness, you will suffer."
He straightened. "Now, let's see if we can relieve some of your
pain. Let's talk about your boss."

"Snowball's chance in Hell."

"So, you want to play it that way? Okay. Answer one thing—
how the hell did you find us in Possum Holler?"

"Google."

~

Brow wrinkled, Tanner slammed the door of his mailbox
shut. He thumbed through the envelopes as he opened the door of
his house. *Bills!* He paused at an ivory envelope addressed in a
delicate script. *Too soon for Dixon's invitation.* Walking into the
house, he tore the seal.

Linked wedding bands adorned the front of the card inside.
The back said:

*This Friday, 3:30. Courthouse. Bring the kids.
Laura Beth will be there. Doug and I are taking the
plunge in our old age.*

Love,
Madeleine

Tanner laughed. "I could use a good oath. I wonder if the
nuns at the orphanage washed Marin's mouth out with soap. It
didn't help."

"Dad!" Tanner's children rushed in the door from the school
bus.

"Hey, troops!" He held up the invitation. "We're invited to Miss Madeleine's wedding."

"Cool," said Roslyn. "Can I dress up?"

"You'll have to wear nice clothes to school. It's this Friday. I'll pick y'all up."

Corbin's face contorted in a frown and a wrinkled nose. Tanner ruffled his hair. "I think khakis and a button-down shirt will do. It's not formal."

"Good," said the boy heading for the refrigerator.

Tanner reached around the child and got a roll of sausage. Corbin grabbed a blended-fruit yogurt. Both turned to the stove where a pot of dry red beans already soaked. Pointing at the yogurt, the father said, "No more snacks. Red beans and rice for supper."

~

Only a handful of friends congregated in the justice of the peace's chambers at the courthouse on Friday as the older couple, both widowed, exchanged vows. The bride wore a simple tailored, light-blue, linen pant suit; the groom, a navy-blue suit with a white shirt and light blue tie.

Madeleine asked Laura Beth to sign as a witness. Doug Blanchard asked, "Detective McGill, would you mind?"

"Not at all, but call me Tanner."

"Where is your family?" asked Laura Beth.

"Scattered," said Madeleine. "We did let our kids know, but we aren't waiting for a time everyone can come."

After the brief ceremony, the couple announced they had reserved the private dining room at Gus's for a celebration and asked the few friends in attendance to meet them there. Madeleine handed the one dyed-blue rosebud she held to Marge Dixon. "I hear you're next anyway."

"Yes, ma'am. You'll be there?"

"I wouldn't miss it, sweetheart."

~

Penny marched into the office Ed Pickering was still using. Tanner sat in a chair in front of the desk. "What's this?" demanded the sheriff. "I feel as if I've been summoned."

Tanner dipped his head back and forth from shoulder to shoulder. "You sort of have."

"What do you want?"

The two men looked at each other.

"I'll let you say it," stated the FBI agent. "Maybe she won't break your neck."

Tanner rubbed both hands fast across his thighs, generating heat in his palms. *Quit stalling McGill. Just say it and get it over with. She'll scream at you no matter what.* "Umm."

"Oh, shit!" exclaimed Penny. "You two want me to try to get Marin to talk because he's supposedly attracted to me." She stormed to the door. "Not a-happening! Men! Damn every last one of you!" She slammed the door so hard the wall shook.

"That went well." Tanner grinned at Pickering.

Pickering scratched his head. "The real problem is that she likes him."

"Don't let her hear you say that."

~

A down-town Victorian home turned into a site for social events hosted Marge Dixon and Luis Montoya's wedding. The couple chose simple vows. Penny served as maid of honor. Surprisingly, Ed Pickering stood beside the young man who had been his son's partner. Animosity between the two men had been put aside. However, the maid of honor glowered at the best man throughout the exchange of vows.

The grounds of the old house hosted the wedding reception. When Tanner stood beside Penny, she growled, "Don't say a word."

"Sorry."

"I took a vow to uphold the law. Making that man, no matter how loathsome, think I could be interested in him just to get information goes beyond entrapment." *Even if he is sexy as hell even with his schnozz. That body is to kill for. And that voice— smooth as silk.*

"Forget it. I'll figure it out." Tanner sipped his punch.

As they talked, the sheriff's cell phone rang. She pulled it from the bosom of the dress she wore—shiny gold, fitted, strapless, mid-thigh length.

Tanner's eyes popped wide and his mouth dropped open.

"What? Stop catching flies!" Ulmer demanded. "Where else in this dress was I supposed to put it? Maybe I should have worn garters so one could hold the phone and the other my gun? I'm still sheriff even out of uniform." Into the phone she said, "I swear this had better be good...Well, shit!" She closed the phone. "It seems Marin has spiked a fever. The shot to his ass has made him sick. He's asking for me. Party's over."

McGill approached Laura Beth and asked if she'd take Corbin and Roslyn with her. She agreed once he explained the situation. He signaled Pickering and the three law enforcers left before the bride and groom.

·22

Up the Ladder

In the parking area of the hospital, McGill said, "You two go see what's up with Marin. I think I was getting close to something with all those hobnobbing pictures I found. I'll call or you call, whichever gets a lead."

Tanner went back to his office and powered up his computer. He looked for any photo that might contain Marin with official personnel. Christmas the year before finally offered hope.

Diego Marin, looking like Secret Service, appeared in a number of photos at a high-powered party. These shots McGill copied and placed in a file. After that event, Marin vanished again.

"Okay," McGill mumbled. "Talk to me." He put the files on a flash drive and headed to the CVS Pharmacy to print and enlarge.

~

Penny Ulmer and Ed Pickering arrived at Marin's room. Although both had been there and Pickering himself had placed the guards, both sheriff and agent had to undergo the rigid security measures.

Ulmer balked at the male guard searching her. "Where in the hell can I hide anything in this dress?" She handed him the gun that was strapped over her chest.

"Bra?"

"Not wearing one, buster!"

"Sorry, Sheriff."

She jabbed a fingernail into the guard's chest. "If your hands linger a split second, I get Marin's katana and amputate them."

"Yes, ma'am."

After a thorough pat-down and leaving their weapons outside, Pickering and Ulmer entered the hospital room.

Marin, still face down, smiled. "Ah, I smell you, Pretty Penny—sweet pea and violet."

The woman clenched her fists.

Marin continued, "But why did you bring that asshole?"

"*His* is intact."

"Ouch. Cold. Play nice."

"How did you know anyone else was here?"

"I smell him too. English Leather, cheap old-school shit."

"Like your Old Spice?" Pickering snapped. "Laura Beth remembered your scent."

"Yeah. I know."

Penny laughed despite her resolve to hate the prisoner.

"You have to help me, Pretty Penny," Marin said.

"Help you?"

"Have you seen the news today?"

"Nope. I've been at Dixon and Montoya's wedding."

"Come closer." He pushed a button and the bed rotated ninety degrees. He was strapped in. He moaned as the act put pressure on his injury. "You are one fine woman. This is the first time I've seen you in a dress. Those legs gone on *forever*."

"Shut up," Pickering barked. "What about the news?"

"Somebody's leaked your suspicions about someone high in government. You have to get me out of here."

"Scared?" asked Ulmer.

"Have you two ever heard of Iran-Contra?"

"Sure."

"It's sort of the same, Pretty Penny. I know I should've questioned orders. Oliver North went to prison. I can't do that, but I did ask questions."

"Too bad."

"Listen up, both of you." His eyes darted around. "No McGill?"

"He's working another angle," Pickering said. "Spit out what you have to say."

"Fine. The administration knew a lot in Iran-Contra, but they weren't evil murderous bitches."

"There you go again," said Penny. "So, are we looking for a woman?"

"Just listen and then spring me." He turned the bed back down. "Just watch CNN. I'm sure they'll play the story again." He moaned. "Sorry about mooning you, but it doesn't hurt as much this way."

"I'm out of here." The sheriff started to leave.

"Wait!"

"You better make it worth my time."

"I was told to find the person sent to eliminate those who put Perez away and information was about to come to light to prove they lied." He took a breath. "He supposedly was supplying info on worse drug lords and even more heinous crimes."

"Worse?" Penny's laugh oozed cynicism.

"Yeah. More powerful. More connected. Working more angles than drugs. Illegals. Missing Americans. Prostitution. Human trafficking. Terrorism. You get the picture?"

"So, you're saying Perez was an informant?" asked Pickering.

Marin tried to shrug. "That's what my boss said, but DEA and FBI brought him down. FBI, Pickering. You and Montoya were on the hit list."

"Why Montoya?"

"Please? I found who I think is pulling strings and got the news to my boss. She knew he was under."

"She?" Penny jumped on the tidbit.

"No mas. Get me out of here if you want more."

Penny and Pickering exchanged looks. The agent splayed his hands, palms up, and shrugged. "Not my call."

"I don't want you to do damned thing for me, Pickering," Marin asserted. "Look how easily I found Little Momma. And you can forget WITSEC. My boss would have no part of that."

"Who's your boss?"

"I work for an agency you know nothing about, Pickering. CIA is a pansy stepsister. Pretty Penny, I need your help." He pushed a button. "I'm going to sleep now. Little Momma shot me in the ass, and it hurts like a bitch."

Within seconds, Marin snored. Penny grumbled, "I thought he spiked a fever."

"He did," said the guard. "They took him to surgery and lanced the abscess." He pointed to the I.V.s. "Some super-duper antibiotic and morphine. He'd been holding off on the M 'til you came, Sheriff."

Penny knitted her arched brows and snarled like a rabid dog.

Yep. She likes him. Pickering dared not utter his thoughts.

~

Tanner sat at his desk staring at a dozen photos in which he had circled Diego Marin. A few appeared to be friendly conversation. Others looked as if he was working as he often had a hand to his ear. Talking aloud to himself, Tanner followed the progression of the man's movements after Marin left a young woman in a sarong and tiara and a much older man wearing a fez.

"Snagging hors d'oeuvres...Swigging champagne." He had to stop and laugh at the roguishness. "I could have liked him. Okay. Moving on. Hand to ear...Deep frown...Bow to gray-haired couple...Hand to ear...Speaking...In the shadows...Female and male in a deep discussion...Hiding just out of their sight." Tanner squinted. "Who are you? You look familiar."

One last picture with Marin in the background and several State Department people at a press conference struck like the lightning bolt that brought Frankenstein's monster to life. One woman sat on the stage. "This is where I remember Marin from. I saw him at the press conference when Perez was arrested." He cropped the picture to show only the woman and saved it to his flash.

The detective read the caption. "Undersecretary of State Margarita Hernandez."

He went back to the picture of Marin eavesdropping on the woman in the shadows, cropped it to show only the three people and rushed back to the pharmacy.

Fifteen minutes later, he slammed the two pictures onto his desk. "Gotcha!"

Tanner Googled images and web information on the undersecretary. One large family photo came up. It was a ninetieth birthday celebration for a twice-removed uncle, a World War II vet—only two years before.

Tanner enlarged each face. He slapped the top of his desk. "Hot damn! They're cousins! Gotcha, bitch! Now I have more questions though. You weren't talking to Marin, but the other guy." *Is Marin telling the truth? Has he been trying to save Laura Beth?*

He saved the photo to his flash and started out the door again.

Ulmer and Pickering walked in. Tanner grinned. "Marin's not the only one who can use Google. I found her! She's Perez's cousin!"

23
Political Upheaval

Pickering snatched the photos. "How do you know?"

Tanner led the other two law enforcers to his desk and showed the progression of his research. He stabbed the old uncle's face. "This man deserves better. Julio Roberto Sanchez-Perez was a war hero. Thank God he passed away just weeks after this birthday, so he never has to know what his relatives are like. Perez's great-grandfather was Julio's younger brother. He was killed at Iwo Jima." Tanner scrolled the write-up. "According to this, Perez was a successful import-export mogul." He laughed. "And we know what his product was."

"More than drugs according to our prisoner." Pickering grunted, "Get into the connection. I have to have something strong. This will cause some serious political upheaval."

"Okay." Tanner clicked a link. "Margarita Elena Martinez-Hernandez is the daughter of Julio's niece, his sister's child. That's why the Perez doesn't show up. His sister was Maria Teresa Sanchez-Perez, married Carlito Ramon Cruz. Their daughter is still living, Linda Cruz-Martinez, married to Pedro Hector Hernandez. Margarita is about ten years older than Perez, but they're third cousins. In Latino families, you're cousins for ten generations."

Penny nodded. "Black families too. And many Southern white families."

"True," Tanner said. "So, this gets a double dose—Latino and Texan."

"Wait a sec." Pickering tapped a picture. "That's McCormick. Marin swears he's the hitman and Marin was sent to stop him and find out about a real terrorist threat high up the chain."

Tanner looked up. "That's the third dead agent from the safe house?"

Pickering nodded.

Scowling, Tanner asked, "Is Marin the fall guy? Was he really trying to help?"

"Could be. He said something about working for a secret agency," Penny informed. "But you've tied him to McCormick and McCormick to this woman. If she *is* a terrorist plant, she's good, and Marin could be in danger."

Tanner arched an eyebrow. Penny shrugged. "He's sort of incapacitated right now. Not real able to defend himself."

Pickering asked, "Can you type this into a coherent report with pictures?"

"Sure," said Tanner. "Give me a couple of hours."

"I have to book a flight. Work fast." Pickering left to use the space he still occupied at the police station.

~

Agent Edward Pickering walked into the office of the head of the FBI. He laid the detailed report on his boss's desk and sat across from his boss without invitation. Rodney Malouf opened the file and read carefully.

"Pickering, do you enjoy making my life hell?"

"You can't blame this one on me. Your taskforce brought Perez down. Now we know how there was so much retaliation."

Pickering tapped Marin's photo. "He's been on some secret payroll for a long time. I don't want to know what all he's done or even who he works for. You just need to get rid of Perez's cousin, Marin's shot-caller with possible terrorist connections. McCormick turned up as an alias. He's so dirty the IRA wouldn't even claim him."

"I'm taking you with me. Secretary Collins is *not* going to be happy."

~

Two hours later, the two FBI representatives enter the office of the Secretary of State. The smartly dressed lady in her sixties stood to greet the men.

"Tell me this is all a horrible mistake," she said, indicating for the two men to sit.

"I'm afraid not," FBI Director, Rodney Malouf said. "Horrible, yes. Mistake, no. Crime, yes. But we can cover State's behind with quick action." He handed her the file.

Secretary Collins read every word of the report before uttering another sound. "This doesn't prove Margarita's involved," she finally stated.

"No, but it's too suspicious not to investigate," argued Malouf.

The Secretary of State ran nervous fingers through short blonde hair. "You're right. I'm putting her on administrative leave pending a full investigation, and I'll hold a press conference first thing in the morning. The sharks will be feeding before I leave the office today."

The Secretary picked up her phone. When the party answered, she said, "Margarita, I need you in my office. Now." She terminated the call.

Then she dialed another number. "I need security. Now." .

~

Margarita Hernandez made one call from a prepaid cell phone before she went to her boss's office. "It's happened. You know what to do." She stopped in the restroom and flushed the tiny phone down the toilet.

A tall Latina with short cropped hair in her early fifties entered the office of the Secretary of State. Armed security stood ready.

Secretary Collins rose with the FBI. She shook her head. "Margarita, I hate to have to do this, but I'm placing you on administrative leave, pending an investigation. Would you like to talk to us?"

"Why?"

"Margarita." She closed her eyes for moment and took a deep breath. "It's come to light that you are cousins with Carlos Perez. You know how bad that must look."

"So, I'm being punished for my bloodline?"

"Did you have anything to do with the deaths of those federal witnesses, not to mention FBI agents?"

Margarita frowned.

Secretary Collins asked, "Why didn't you tell me about your relationship?"

"Isn't it obvious?" The woman looked around the room. "I didn't want this to happen."

"If you had been forthcoming, it wouldn't have. Therefore, I must be suspicious. I need your I.D. and your computer access. You will leave the premises and not return for anything. You will not leave the area. You will be watched. You're suspended with pay—for now." Collins nodded to the security officers who approached Margarita.

The undersecretary snapped, "Don't touch me." She slammed the items that had been requested onto her boss's desk, turned on her heel and walked out, head held high.

~

Early the next morning, Diego Marin turned on the TV in his hospital room. Finally able to lie in a normal position, he looked forward to breakfast. Secretary Collins's televised press conference grabbed his attention:

> *Undersecretary of State Margarita Hernandez has been placed on administrative leave with pay, pending investigation into illegal involvement with her now-known cousin, Carlos Perez.*

"Shit!" He did not listen to the rest of the news as his in-room guard came out the restroom. "Get me Penny Ulmer. Now!" His voice could be heard at the nurse's station.

24

Argentine Asylum

Sheriff Penny Ulmer poured a bowl of raisin bran, snagged toast as it popped up, slathered it with butter and apple jelly and poured a cup of steaming coffee. She took a sip of black coffee then a bite of toast. "Mmm."

She flicked on a small TV to catch the daily weather and almost choked on her first spoon of cereal as she listened to the press conference that was the lead on *Good Morning, America.*

Anticipating the first leisurely breakfast she'd had in months, the sheriff snarled when her phone rang. "What do you want, Marin?"

"Well, it's Officer Murray, Sheriff, but I am calling for Diego."

"Diego?" Her voice came out shrill. "You're on a fist-name basis with that snake?"

"Here. Talk to him."

Before she could protest, Marin's voice said, "Pretty Penny, help me. Have you seen the news this morning?"

"Yep."

"Please, Pretty Penny?"

"Tell you what—I'll come babysit you."

"They'll kill you too. That would upset me."

"Oh, shut up!" She terminated the call, got dressed and drove to the hospital.

~

Her stomach growling protest at not being filled, Penny stopped and purchased breakfast for two at McDonald's on her way to the medical center. *I must be nuts.*

The sheriff walked up to Marin's room as a nurses' aide delivered breakfast, but only one tray. *I thought they fed the guards. This feels real off.*

Penny stood beside the woman as the guard reviewed his list. "Sorry, Miss, but you aren't on the list. Where's Yolanda?"

"She called out sick. They called me this morning."

"What's Marin having for breakfast?" asked Penny.

"I'm not sure." The young girl lifted the cover from the plate. "Grits, scrambled eggs, juice and coffee. He's still on a soft diet."

"Uh-huh." Penny frowned. "Take it back."

"What?"

"He's not eating that."

The guard eyed the McDonald's bag. Penny followed his eyes. She smiled. "I brought Marin's breakfast, but you didn't bring anything for the guards." She shot the girl a stern glare.

"They just changed shifts."

"Okay. Take the food back."

The girl scowled. "On second thought," said Penny, "give me the tray."

The aide handed the food to the sheriff. She set it on the table by the guard. She took off her weapon and lifted her arms to be searched. The girl stomped off. The guard waved Penny in. She pointed to the tray. "Don't touch that. I think it's poisoned. Take it to the lab—now."

"But..."

"NOW!" She opened the door. "Murray, take the post outside."

Murray stepped out. "What's up?"

"Thompson has to go to the lab. Tell them I said to rush it."

"Yes, ma'am," said Thompson, taking the breakfast tray.

"Oh," Penny called, "if that little girl comes near you, shoot her."

Thompson nodded and Murray took up his position. Penny stepped in with the breakfast from McDonald's.

~

Marin raised his bed. "Bearing gifts?"

"Shut up." She dragged the hospital tray over Marin's lap and pulled two big breakfasts from the bag. She put them with coffee and orange juice on the rolling table and placed the guard's chair beside the bed. "You interrupted my breakfast."

"I don't care about food."

"Really?" She poured syrup over the hotcakes.

"Pretty Penny!"

"Mmm," she moaned around a mouthful.

"Damn it! I'm a dead man. That crazy bitch will think I ratted her out, but I wasn't even sure she was the one."

"By crazy bitch, do you mean Undersecretary of State Margarita Hernandez?"

"Yes!" He struck his mattress with is fist. "Are you happy now? I needed hard evidence."

Penny retrieved a recorder from the pocket of her trousers. "Talk to me." She pointed with a plastic fork. "And eat. It's not poisoned."

Diego tentatively took a bite of the eggs in the meal. "Got ketchup?" His voice sounded pouty.

Penny laughed out loud. She reached in the bag and handed the prisoner ketchup packets. "I like ketchup on my scrambled eggs too."

"What did you mean about the poison?"

She swallowed. "I think you had a little hitchick outside. She wasn't the normal aide. I sent her packing and the food to the lab."

"So? You believe me?"

"Yeah. About that."

They ate for a few minutes in silence. Penny pushed her plate back. "I'm stuffed. Now, talk to me." She pressed the record button.

Marin poured creamer into his coffee and took a big gulp.

"I've worked covert ops as an assassin for over ten years. I've also done a number of extractions and most recently I've been trying to discover who with top ties also has terrorist ties. My orders have always come from a CIA operative that works for one of their most guarded offshoots. You'd be surprised who our government wants bumped off, and I usually never got a reason."

Penny scowled. "And you never questioned orders?" She tilted her head to one side.

"This is my country. I swore an oath to protect her from all enemies, both foreign and domestic. I drew the line on children. What could they possibly have done to be a political enemy?"

"You ran Laura Beth off the road with her children in the car." The sheriff arched her eyebrow high.

Marin shook his head. "That little depression at her snail speed wasn't dangerous."

"Go on."

"I had never been given an assignment on American soil before I was ordered to work security at that big party with lots of foreign dignitaries. I was told I'd receive my new assignment there. That's when I spotted McCormick, who I'd already fingered as having terrorist connections, posing as more security. I saw him meet with Undersecretary Margarita Hernandez. She gave him a list and told him the witnesses had lied and that Carlos Perez had to be freed because he was helping bring down

Mexican drug cartels. McCormick had to find and eliminate five federal witnesses." He finished his coffee.

"I did question operating domestically with my boss, but I was told this was top priority. The expression on Hernandez's face told me there was already a laser target on my forehead if I didn't find proof that she was the party we were after. It was only a matter of time before they sent someone after me because I was no longer just a shadow. That's when I decided this was it. No more. My boss told me this could be my last case."

He pushed the rolling table away from the bed. "Bathroom break."

Penny stood. "Do you need a hand?"

"No. I've got it." He shuffled to the bathroom, rolling his I.V. and his hospital gown showing his backside. The shackles on his feet made moving difficult although his wrists had been freed.

"When will they let you wear underwear?" Penny mumbled behind him.

"I never wear underwear," Marin replied over his shoulder.

When he returned and slid gingerly back into bed, Penny resumed her interrogation. "Tell me about Laura Beth."

"I never expected her. I slipped up, not anticipating the census when I followed McCormick. He contacted Hernandez and she told him to make sure Laura Beth didn't talk. I only planned to scare her, but when she started working with the cops, she became the target. It seemed McCormick kept a step ahead of me. I got to Perez's apartment minutes after she was killed. Little Momma saw me leaving, but I didn't kill the woman. Again, I questioned and was given to understand I had no say in the matter and if I didn't comply, I might end up dead. I discovered the list had added Montoya and Pickering. I called my boss and gave him all I had. He gave me the green light to try to stage Laura Beth's death." He grabbed Penny's cup and drank some of her coffee. She gave him a dirty look and he passed the cup back. Penny wrinkled her nose, got up, and poured the rest of her coffee down the sink.

Marin laughed out loud. "I confronted McCormick and told him *his* boss wasn't happy. We went to the strip club where he picked up a chick and left with her. He had grumbled about not being able to get to Laura Beth and talked about killing Montoya while he was on watch. I told him I'd take his head if he did. And I told him to knock Montoya out. Um, even I didn't expect Dixon to show up. I rigged the car to blow up, but nobody was supposed to be in it. I had watched several days. I didn't count on the good doctor taking the car to the rental place. I even tried to call Secretary Collins. I was put on hold. Check phone records."

"Really?"

He nodded.

"Speak," she said, pointing at the recorder. "It doesn't hear your brains rattling in your head."

"Yes. I planned to tell Cline and Kilpatrick the whole story and take Little Momma myself somewhere safe. I thought I could fake her death." He pointed at her. "And I know I made it sound like I wanted to nail her before I killed her, but I thought if I frightened her enough, she'd fall into line and I could actually save her. I had no intention of forcing myself on her. She is some little spitfire! That damned perfume in the eyes was worse than pepper spray."

"Right." Penny gave him a lopsided smirk.

"I'm telling the truth. McCormick went into the room and I knew something was up. I followed and broke through the door just as Cline's head hit the ground. I reacted and killed McCormick."

"But you killed the stripper as if she was nothing?"

Marin rubbed his hands across his face. "I didn't kill the woman. McCormick did. To him, she was just collateral damage.

I just helped get rid of the evidence trying to win his confidence. The stupid woman should have chosen her johns better."

Penny ground her teeth, widened her eyes and fisted her hands.

"Okay. Sorry." Marin held up his hands as if in surrender.

"And Bruce Copeland?"

"Nobody was supposed to be in the damned car. How many times do I have to say it? The good doctor left every morning at seven. I rigged a timer for the car to blow up at seven-thirty, after he was gone in *his* Mercedes. Little Momma would not have left to go anywhere that early. She let her little ones sleep. She's a good mother."

Penny snorted. "You met your match with Laura Beth."

"Nope. That'd be you." He grinned.

"Oh, shut up."

~

Mid-morning, Marin's doctor came in. Penny had to stay under the circumstances.

The doctor nodded with satisfaction. "I think we can lose the I.V."

Penny interrupted. "Who took off the cuffs?"

"I did. For surgery. The ankle manacles were off too at the time." The doctor sounded angry.

"Doc, you do realize Mr. Marin is a ruthless killer, right?"

"So, I've been told."

"When can he be transferred to a maximum-security federal prison?"

"Soon." The doctor turned to go. "I'll send the nurse to remove the I.V." He left.

Marin glared at Penny. "You know she'll have me killed."

"You're a master martial artist. You can defend yourself." She gave him a cold, unfeeling stare.

As Diego started to speak, Penny's phone rang. "Yeah. Talk to me, Phil...Cyanide..." She made eye contact with the prisoner. "Enough to kill a horse...Thanks." She closed her phone.

Diego started to speak again. The sheriff shook her head. She dialed Pickering and related the morning's incident. They heard voices outside. Penny terminated the call and opened the door.

The aide from earlier argued with the guard that she was there to remove Marin's I.V. *Aides aren't certified for that.* Penny cleared her throat. "It's all good, Murray."

"But..." He pointed at the list.

"I know."

"It's on you, Sheriff."

"I know that too."

The young woman grinned triumphantly and stepped inside the room. Penny closed the door, whipped handcuffs off her belt and pinned the woman's wrists behind her, clamping them tight. The sheriff snatched a washcloth from the bedside table and stuffed it in the woman's mouth.

"I have a few questions for you. Nods will suffice. Are you here to kill Marin?"

The girl's eyes grew wide.

"Good enough answer. Marin, get out of bed."

The man obeyed, his hospital gown opening to reveal all his glory.

Penny shoved the other assassin into the bed. She took a second pair of handcuffs and secured the new prisoner to the bed railing.

She turned to Marin and with very little care, ripped the tape and tubing of the I.V. from the man's hand. He yelped.

"Shut up." She took a key from her pocket and unlocked the foot fetters. She called loudly, "Murray, I need you in here."

The guard stepped in and surveyed the room. "I'll explain it all later. Marin needs your uniform."

"Ma'am?"

"He doesn't wear underwear, so you won't be naked." She pointed to the girl. "Hitwoman. Give Marin your clothes. Give us ten minutes and call Pickering."

Murray complied with great reluctance.

~

Laura Beth watched a CNN news report near midnight. A plane had apparently crashed in the jungle in South America. A strange tingling ran down her spine.

Two days later, Enrique de la Vega, Spanish oil mogul, stepped off a plane in Buenos Aries. His personal limousine transported him further. He entered a heavily guarded compound where a Mediterranean villa surrounded by botanical gardens awaited.

25

Housewarming

Laura Beth opened her front door to find three law enforcement officers. "What now?" She demanded.

"May we come in?" Tanner asked.

Laura Beth scowled. "With all of you here, it has to be bad news." She stepped back. "Come in. Coffee?"

"No. We're fine," Tanner said.

She ushered McGill, Pickering and Ulmer into the living room. "Please have a seat."

Once all were settled, Pickering began, "Mrs. Copeland, we have to let you know Diego Marin has, um, disappeared."

"Uh-huh? And you know exactly where he is, right?"

Pickering fidgeted. Laura Beth continued, "Let me guess. Witness protection. He finally gave up his boss."

"Well, yes and no."

Laura Beth shot up from her chair. "Well, just great! A cold-blooded murderer is free just so you can go up the ladder!"

"Sugar..." Tanner began.

Stopping his comment, she pointed at him. "Don't even go there. I get it. This Hernandez person might be worse because she gave the orders and is suspected of terrorist connections. I saw CNN. Still, that man murdered my husband." She marched to the front door. "Out! All of you."

Pickering spoke. "He's not even in this country anymore. You're safe."

"Yeah. Thanks a million. I'm a widow at thirty with three children. Bruce had good insurance, but I still have to go back to work when I wanted to wait until all my children were in school. I'm testing next week for my realtor's license. I have to get my life on an even keel. How could you do this to me, Agent Pickering?"

"He didn't. I did," Penny said. "I sprang Marin for good reasons."

"Good reasons? I thought you were my friend."

"I am. Let me explain."

"No! I couldn't care less about Diego Marin. May he rot in a mosquito infested jungle! Right now, all of you can join him."

Penny clenched her fists. "He's dead, Laura Beth. Didn't you see the news? His plane crashed."

"Is he really?"

"I don't know." Penny's voice broke.

"My God! You're worried he's actually dead. Get out!" The shrillness of Laura Beth's voice showed her pure rage.

The three law enforcers left. Tanner paused. "Not my call, Sugar."

"I hear you." A slight smile flickered across her lips. "They brought you to soften the blow. My friend"—She shook her head—"Penny stabbed me in the back. You can call me."

Tanner squeezed her hand and followed the other two officers. He knew Pickering had brought him to try to make breaking the news easier. He breathed in relief that Laura Beth accepted that he was not involved in the decision to spirit Marin away, yet he felt a pang of pity for Penny. *It was a hard choice for her.*

~

Laura Beth rubbed her forehead as she finished her test for a real estate license. "Now I wait," she muttered.

Outside the testing center, she pulled out her phone and texted Tanner McGill. "Done. Buy me a burger?"

A return message popped unto her screen. "Gus's. Half an hour."

They arrived within seconds of each other and parked side by side. "How was it?" Tanner asked.

"Piece of cake. Still, I have to wait."

"How's Stacey liking kindergarten?"

"She loves it. Is Corbin enjoying middle school?"

Tanner laughed. "He complains every day, but he's doing well. He doesn't think the instructors care as much as his elementary teachers. I think he gets that it's the fact that he only spends and hour a day with each of them that makes it feel less personal."

They entered the café and took a booth near the back. When Gus himself came to take care of them, Laura Beth ordered a cheeseburger while Tanner got the house special. After sipping her Coke, Laura Beth asked, "Any news on Marin and others?"

"There's a federal investigation into Hernandez. Last I heard, they were bringing charges. She's currently under house arrest at her home in Texas. Perez won't be getting out. I hope I never hear from Marin again."

"Don't count on that one. Do you know where he is? Is he really dead?"

"I doubt it. My guess is somewhere in Argentina."

She nodded. "He's scot-free."

"Maybe, but I'd put money on Pickering having him watched twenty-four/seven; just to make sure he doesn't come back, if he has that authority."

They stopped talking as their food arrived. Once the server who brought their order moved on, Tanner finished, "And Uncle Sam might still have him on payroll. Pickering said it was not Federal Marshals that met them at the airport, and it appeared Marin knew one of them. Keep tuned to the news to see if any known drug cartel leaders bite the dust."

"You're serious."

He chugged some tea. "Whew! That's spicy," he said of his goulash. "Yes, I am. Still, he's out of our hair, and a real threat is going down. Marin never would have come after you if he hadn't been ordered to." He held up a hand as she started to speak. "That doesn't excuse his actions, but he's so indoctrinated, his own judgment was clouded, and, believe it or not, I think he was doing what he could to keep you safe. He was working to find who was calling the shots."

"I guess." She sighed.

Tanner deftly changed the subject. "How's my little man doing?"

"He's sitting up."

"I'd like to see him."

"Bring the kids and let's have a cookout Saturday. I'll invite a few other friends. We'll have a little party."

"Penny?"

Laura Beth frowned. "I guess I should stop being mad at her."

"Yep, Sugar, you should. Life is too short to hold grudges. She did what she thought was best for all."

"Okay. I'll ask her too." She sighed. "She has feelings for that bastard."

"She needs her friend to understand." He placed a gentle hand on top of hers across the table.

~

Saturday afternoon, Laura Beth had a houseful of friends. Penny Ulmer brought a carrot cake made from two bunt cakes placed together and the frosting dyed orange and decorated with candy corns for a jack-o-lantern face as a peace offering.

Laura Beth took the cake and smiled. "Sorry," said Penny, "but it was the lesser of two evils."

"I'm really trying to understand, but I feel as if you stabbed me in the back. Honestly, I don't know if I can ever get back to where we once were." She set the cake on the desert table. "I suppose Hernandez could have been a real terrorist."

"Exactly. And she was trying to have Ninja Man killed— might have succeeded."

"He became a liability." Laura Beth shrugged. "I wouldn't have shed tears, but I sure hope she gets hers. Yet, I don't think Diego Marin had any balls cowering before that woman."

"Oh, he had balls and a bat to match."

"What?"

"Never mind." The sheriff shook her head and waved her hand simultaneously. "I just want to try to rebuild our friendship."

~

A few days later, Laura Beth received her realtor's license in the mail. She smiled and called a friend who owned a real estate company. Peg Shriver said jovially, "Welcome aboard. We'll start you in the office, receptionist sort of. In a few weeks, you can show your first house."

Laura Beth breathed easier and called Madeleine. The older woman clapped happily. She had agreed to babysit for Laura Beth for a nominal fee.

The same day Laura Beth opened an envelope with her new employment secured, Penny Ulmer found a large package left at her front door. It was covered with international stamps.

"Oh, shit!" she groaned. "He's alive. That man is a fool."

Lifting the box, Penny felt it weighed a great deal. She knitted her eyebrows together. She sighed as she sat on her sofa.

For several minutes she drummed her fingers on the package, considering just sending it back.

Tentatively, she slipped a finger under the end of the flap of the brown paper. She shrugged. *What the hell?*

With great care she removed the wrapping and lifted the cover of the box. Two envelopes lay on top of tissue covering something. She opened the thinner one to find a simple ivory card. Inside was a note:

Hey, Pretty Penny,

First, thanks—for everything. I wish I had met you years ago. I think I would have returned to a small town in Mississippi long before all the shit came down. I still wonder if that caramel skin of yours tastes as sweet as it looks. Maybe one day I'll find out.

I know—I'm shutting up. I sent you pictures of my new home and a little gift. Enjoy.

Enrique de la Vega

Aka Ninja Man ☺

Penny opened the second envelope. A dozen pictures were inside a folded piece of paper. A scrawled note said:

Not sure if those scopes are pointed toward me or away from me. Should I feel safe or scared shitless? At least two of my new friends accompany me wherever I go. I can't really explain who Enrique de la Vega is. My boss would flay me.

Pictures of the villa showed its opulence—marble tile, parquet floors, crystal lighting, Olympic-sized pool, dojo with padded floors and walls. "Nice," she murmured.

The whole place was surrounded by a high stone wall topped with razor wire and what appeared to be an electrified wire running through it. Guards armed with sniper rifles, side arms and other weapons sat in four towers at each corner of the grounds, which otherwise sported pristine landscaping. Other photos showed a number of guards on patrol. Six smaller dwellings dotted the grounds—*live-in security*, she thought. *A prison of your own making, or is this just setting you up to be another actor in another dark comedy?*

Penny lifted the folds of tissue to find a set of nunchucks and a bo in two parts that could be assembled, both etched with identical serpentine carvings as Marin's sword. She shivered. One of the photos showed the sword on the dojo wall. *He really thinks we're a match. Am I that cold and calculating? Maybe I'm the opposite and that's what he sees. Oh, shit!* She rubbed her face with both hands. *Here I am thinking about that snake—that magnificent specimen of a yowza! Stop it, Penny.* She sighed. *Maybe he's not as evil as he appeared. Please, God, don't let me like Satan's spawn. Let him be a good guy.*

She pulled the bo from the box and assembled it. Standing, she gave it a few swings. It was exactly the right length and the perfect weight for her. She picked up the nunchucks. They were made of obsidian. She performed some signature moves with the martial arts weapon she mastered. She shook her head. *Another time and another place—maybe.*

She returned the weapons to the box, opened her back door and gave a shrill whistle. From the back of the wooded property that bordered the Copeland property, two Great Danes, one black and one tawny, large enough to look like ponies, ran full speed to their mistress's summons. She rubbed both dogs behind the ears. "Come in, babies. Momma's in a funk."

~

For the first two weeks of December, Laura Beth answered phones at Sun Realty. Early one morning as she was alone, she answered the chiming device.

Before she offered the standard greeting, a cheerful voice said, "Laura Beth, Marge Montoya here."

"Well, hello. It's been a while."

"Sure has. I'm standing on Shady Oak. Sun just listed this old Victorian. I've always wanted this house, even as a little girl. Can you show it to me right now?"

"Nobody is in the office."

"What if I guarantee an offer?"

"My first sale?" She snatched a Post-it and scribbled a note. "I'm on my way." She stuck the message on her boss's door and left.

Laura Beth arrived to see Marge's unmarked patrol car and that she had been joined by her husband, Luis. The realtor bounced up the sidewalk.

The two women greeted each other with a hug. Luis offered one too, and Laura Beth gladly accepted.

"Is it just going to be a money pit?" he asked with a wry grin.

"I don't think so," answered Laura Beth. "Old Mrs. Conway kept it in good shape. She only has one daughter living and she's in California. She doesn't plan to move back, so make a good offer and I bet she'll bite."

Laura Beth opened the lock box and got the key. She ushered the couple in. "Offer a bit more and you might get the furniture too."

Marge walked through taking in every inch of the place. She ran her hand along the fireplace mantel. "Nothing has changed. I came here once when I was twelve. We came caroling with the church choir." Marge laughed. "Mrs. Conway served all of us wassail. I think I was on my third cup when the pastor realized it was 'real' wassail—rum and all."

Laura Beth popped a hand over her mouth not to laugh loudly. "Was it Pastor Hodge?"

Marge nodded. "Rather than chide the old lady, he just wished her a merry Christmas and hustled us kids out. I love wassail."

Luis chortled. "I've never had it. You'll have to make some in our new kitchen."

They accompanied Laura Beth back to the office where her boss now waited. She grinned at the management and showed Marge and Luis to chairs. They made an offer and Laura Beth called Conway's daughter in California. Fifteen minutes later, the Montoyas left to visit the bank.

Laura Beth sent a text to Tanner McGill. "Lunch? I made my first sale."

"Sure. Pizza? On you?" came the reply.

"Meet you at Papa's."

~

"So, who did you charm into throwing money away?" Tanner asked when Laura Beth got out of her car.

"Luis and Marge."

"Really?" He opened the door to Papa Paul's Pizzeria. "So, they're getting out of the apartment. Which house?"

"Old Mrs. Conway's on Shady Oak."

"I love that house. It suits Marge. Should I throw a housewarming?"

"What a great idea. I'll help."

"Does this mean you're good with spending time with me?"

"Yeah. You're good people, Tanner McGill."

"I'm glad you think so. I'll come over and we can go somewhere to plan some fun for the newlyweds."

"Sounds like a plan."

~

The day Marge and Luis brought their first box of belongings into their new home, they were met by a loud, "Surprise!"

Tanner had thrown together a quick housewarming, and Laura Beth, still having a key to the property, had sneaked in and decorated. Police officers not on duty, along with many other friends Laura Beth had contacted, showered the couple with gifts.

Marge cornered her boss. "Was this your idea?"

"Yes, but I had help." He cut his eyes toward Laura Beth.

"Are things moving the direction you'd like with her?"

He shrugged. "I'm hesitant to push."

"Well, Boss, the general consensus is that you two would be a great couple."

"Thanks." He smirked. "Glad to know I'm the topic of gossip."

Marge held up both hands. "Not so. But your looks are not so subtle to those of us who know you. Thanks for the little party. It's nice to feel appreciated."

Tanner chuckled. "Tomorrow, I give you double work." He walked away to speak to Laura Beth.

26
Man's Best Friend

After a successful housewarming for his assistant, just at dusk on a mid-December day, Tanner arrived at Laura Beth's front door for a dinner date, just as good friends with no strings attached. He knocked and heard two little girls arguing over who should get to answer.

"Stop!" Laura Beth's voice rang out. The door opened.

"Well, merry Christmas," he said with a grin. "I see you already have a wreath up."

"Of course. It's only two more weeks until Christmas. We traditionally do an advent calendar beginning December first. I'm aiming for normalcy," she finished with a sad smile.

"Yes, as you should. I guess I'm a little behind with my decorating. The last couple of years, I've waited for the kids to start Christmas vacation. We do it together."

Both girls still danced without speaking, waiting for a greeting. Tanner smirked. "Well, it is that season. Mrs. Copeland, Santa asked me to make an early delivery. He didn't think it wise to keep this gift at the North Pole until Christmas."

Laura Beth knitted her eyebrows. "What have you done?"

Touching his chest, Tanner said, "I? *Nothing.*"

The mother set her lips in a firm line. *How do I refuse a Santa request in front of the girls? Oh, you're gonna pay.* Through a fake smile she said, "Well, of course. What did Santa send?"

Tanner motioned for the girls. "Come on."

They ran with him to his car. Pacing back and forth in the backseat was a mahogany and brindled puppy about four months old. Laura Beth cautiously followed the trio with a call over her shoulder to Madeleine, who had agreed to babysit later and have her spouse meet her at Laura Beth's house.

"Oh, my God!" Laura Beth muttered. "What have you done? That's a"—She ground her teeth—"Pitbull."

Tanner nodded. "Santa rescued his pregnant mother from a fighting ring. He has three sisters, but the mother..." He trailed off. A sly smile played around his mouth. He said softly, "His mother went to be with your daddy."

Laura Beth stifled a sob. Tanner explained further. "They were all bottle fed. The three girls are being trained as police ladies." He got the puppy from the backseat. "This little guy has a bit of scoliosis. He can't be a police dog. Santa thought he'd fit right in here. He's brave and will protect this house with his life." He locked eyes with Laura Beth. "I'll personally train him."

Laura Beth took several breaths as the girls fawned over the dog. She squinted, her eyes mere slits, at Tanner. "It's a *Pitbull*."

"Gentle as a lamb unless trained otherwise."

"Which you plan to do."

"Not so. He's just in case any *Diegos* should show up."

"What should we name him?" asked Tonya.

"Polka Dot," said Stacey.

"Polka Dot!" Laura Beth and Tanner said together.

"He's got dots all over him," the little girl said.

"But he's a boy," Tanner said. "Polka Dot sounds like a girl." The detective leaned the animal toward Laura Beth. The puppy yipped and licked her face.

"I'll get you for this," she muttered. "How about Spangle?"

"Spangle?" the girls chirped.

"Not bad," Tanner mused. "It means sprinkled or studded with small, bright pieces, objects, spots, etcetera—like The Star Spangled Banner. He is sort of sprinkled with spots."

"Or Freckles," said Madeleine, joining the group with baby Riker on her hip.

The girls looked at each other. "Freckles!" They jumped up and down and clapped.

Tanner turned the puppy to face him. "Freckles? What do you think?"

The dog's tail thumped back and forth, and he barked a squeaky puppy yap.

Tanner laughed. "He hasn't found his voice yet, but I think he likes Freckles."

He put Freckles down and the puppy relieved himself before he began to jump around like a jackrabbit with the girls. The children squealed and laughed. The dog yipped.

The detective grinned. "He's already housebroken."

Laura Beth turned to Tanner after watching the joyous frolicking for a moment. "For this, I'm making you take me somewhere expensive for dinner. You might be unable to afford Christmas gifts for your family."

"As the lady wishes." He opened her door and she waved to the girls.

As they drove down the driveway, Tanner said, "Maybe I had ulterior motives with man's best friend."

Laura Beth raised her eyebrows in question.

Tanner beamed, his dimples showing. "If I train him, I have a good excuse to come around frequently."

Brown eyes looked into his blue ones. There was no joking in them.

She folded her hands in her lap and looked at them, her wedding ring catching the light. She twisted it around her finger. Barely above a whisper, she said, "You don't need an excuse."

27

A Pretty Penny

Laura Beth looked up from the computer screen as the door to the real estate office opened. She frowned. "Out of your jurisdiction, aren't you, Sheriff?"

Penny said, "That depends on whether my friend is *really* ready to forgive me."

Bumping the heels of her hands against the desk, Laura Beth pushed back in her rolling chair. "Why did you do it, Penny? Why did you set him free? I'm still struggling with it."

"He's not free, and he's alive."

"Argentina? The plan crash was just a cover."

"Yes, but I didn't know that. He sent me a gift and pictures. The compound he's in is his prison. The armed guards are as much to keep him in as to keep a threat to him out, and he's still bound to whatever organization employed him. They will milk him dry. Laura Beth, believe it or not, Marin really believes he was doing the right thing."

"To kill Bruce?"

"The last I spoke with Marin, he expressed sincere remorse for that. He was genuinely scared. When the government decides to sanction a hit on one of their own operatives, it happens, even if the shot caller is the real evil one. Investigation has shown Margarita Hernandez to be more of the mastermind with illegal activity than Carlos Perez. She's responsible for the deaths of numerous Mexican citizens, Federales, DEA personnel, and some American tourists. *And* human trafficking—little children being sold into slavery, many as sex slaves." She released a weighted sigh. "Not to mention the communication uncovered with at least three terrorist cells."

Laura Beth scowled. "Penny, do I detect some weird—maybe fatal—attraction to that monster?"

Penny sighed. She pointed at a chair.

Laura Beth nodded. Penny pulled a chair in front of Laura Beth's desk and sat down.

"I don't think he's a monster. He's never had a real family." She massaged the back of her neck. "I think he's afraid of being hurt—his heart, not physically." The sheriff rubbed her hands down both cheeks. "Laura Beth, I'm thirty-nine. I've never been married. I'm not gay. Until I was sexually harassed and assaulted by my commanding officer, I'd planned a military career. The jerk was dishonorably discharged, but I sort of swore off men for a long time." She took several deep breaths. "I live alone with two Great Danes. I'm afraid of being hurt."

Laura Beth sensed her friend's predicament. She said, "Dogs are good companions—always loyal. Tanner just gave the girls a Pitbull puppy, another really big dog, for protection he said."

Penny smiled. "They're great dogs when properly trained. I bet Tanner has volunteered his services as trainer."

"Yeah." Laura Beth relaxed in the presence of her friend. "Tell me about Marin."

"Laura Beth, he's the first man who's called me pretty in years."

"Pretty Penny. I heard."

The sheriff laughed. "Yes. And you didn't see his package."

"Penny!"

"I did. Oh, my God!"

"Is this your libido talking?"

"It's been a long time." She shrugged. "I really dug into Marin's past. Orphan. Parents might have been illegal immigrants from Mexico, but he was apparently born in Texas. Raised by nuns. Joined the military at eighteen. Purple Heart. Congressional Medal of Honor. Beaucoups of secret missions that nobody will reveal. If they find Bin Laden, Marin might get the contract. Yet, he has also rescued political prisoners, hostages, and helped with more than one disaster relief. As far as I can find out, the only murder he's committed without orders from someone he thought was acting in the best interest of the U.S. is Bruce, and that was an accident of a sort." She held up a hand. "I know Bruce was a huge mistake. The bomb experts verified the timer Marin said he used. He didn't expect Bruce to take the car. I can't tell you how sorry I am, but there's something about Diego Marin that's"—She took a breath—"Endearing. Nonetheless, he's gone, and I miss your and my friendship."

Laura Beth pushed her long red hair back from her face. "The heart is a fickle bitch. Penny, I think you're in love with him."

"It doesn't matter."

"Love? Yeah, it matters." She gave the sheriff a lopsided smile. "When do you quit mourning?"

"Are we talking about my man troubles or Tanner McGill?"

Her shoulders touched her ears as Laura Beth shrugged. "I don't know, but I don't think you've heard the last of Diego Marin, Pretty Penny. Do you have Christmas plans?"

"No."

"Come for dinner. We'll eat about two."

"I'd love to."

~

Penny jogged up to her rustic country home with her two dogs in tow. Leather, a black Great Dane with a white stripe down his nose between the eyes, and Lace, an almost immeasurably smaller tawny female with blue eyes, barked and snarled protectively at the person who stood on the porch.

"May I help you?" The sheriff called over the barking. "Quiet!"

The man turned to the homeowner who had just noticed the floral delivery truck. He said, "I have a delivery for Pretty Penny."

"What the hell!"

"Hey, I'll take it back."

"No, you won't." She held her hands out.

The delivery man handed her a potted plant with a single blood-red bloom. The blossom bore an uncanny resemblance to female genitalia.

"Sign here, please," the delivery man said.

Penny signed. "Wait. Tip."

"Taken care of. Night."

Penny unlocked her door and shooed the two dogs inside. She shrugged out of her light-weight jacket as she placed the plant on a table by the door. She twittered and her fingers trembled as she opened the envelope to read a typed card:

A singular bloom for a beautiful blossom. Since I'm relatively close to the beach, I have these growing in my very own botanical gardens in a sandy plot. Plant this one and think of me. It's called Helicodoiceros muscivorus and is a champion of survival. It's native to the Tyrrhenian region: the Balearic Islands, Corsica and Sardinia, always near colonies of gulls. I listen to the haunting cry of the seagulls as they venture near, and then I hear your voice in my head.

I see the plan and think how much I'd like to see the part it looks like on you. No fair! You've seen mine. Show me yours. I miss you, Pretty Penny.

Ninja Man

"You fool!" Penny grumbled. "What if they track you?" *You at least need to wait until that crazy woman is in prison.*

She picked up her phone and dialed a number. When the party answered she said, "Laura Beth, you were right. He just sent me a potted plant, and I swear to God the bloom looks like a pussy."

~

A few days later, the same delivery man showed up at the sheriff's office with a baker's dozen of roses in a most unusual copper color. Penny accepted the delivery.

Again, she read the accompanying card:

I call them "Pretty Pennies." I created them in my own greenhouse. You inspired me. I miss you. How I'd love to hear you tell me to shut up.

Ninja Man

Penny inhaled the sweet fragrance. "Why are you stalking me? You're gonna get yourself killed." She scowled. *Why do I think you're perfectly safe? Your organization has your ass covered.*

~

Christmas Eve, Penny bathed her two canines and tied a red bow on Leather and a green bow on Lace. "Merry Christmas, babies."

Her doorbell rang. She heaved a sigh. "What this time? Poinsettias?"

She turned to her companions. "Stay," and went to the door. There was no floral delivery guy, but a UPS delivery man.

"Sheriff Ulmer," the man greeted with a dip of his head.

"Kincaid."

He handed her a package and a clipboard to sign. With everything in place, he said, "Merry Christmas," and started to his vehicle.

"Merry Christmas," she replied in distracted voice.

Penny closed the door. "I got a gift," she said to the dogs. "Should I open it?"

Both animals barked and wagged their tails. She took it to be an affirmative response.

She sat on her sofa and ripped off the brown paper. Inside, a long, slender box was wrapped in paper sporting candy canes. She tore off that wrap, lifted the lid and separated the red and green tissue.

"Oh, my God! How exquisite!" She took two swords from the box to examine them. The wakizashi and then the tanto were works of art. They were engraved exactly like Diego Marin's katana.

She picked up a card that was inside the box and opened it. The Grinch looked up at her. She chuckled. *He does have a sense of humor. But what's wrong with being a Grinch? His heart grew and he became a new creature with lots of love to give. Is that what Marin is hinting? Is he a new creature with a big heart?* In his neat handwriting, inside read:

Merry Christmas. I thought I'd send you matching serpents and maybe they'd tempt you a little. You have no idea how much this snake would like to slither through your grass—how much this serpent's tongue would like to flick all over you. Damn! I'm getting a hard-on thinking about it. Unfortunately, I'll have to take care of my own issues. I wish you were standing beneath mistletoe near me. I'd kiss you all over.

Merry Christmas,
Much love,
Ninja Man

Penny looked around at her unusual potted plant and back at her exotic and expensive gift. She pulled the blades from their sheaths. They were perfectly weighted for her wrists and the grips fit her hands precisely.

"Damn you, Diego Marin! Why couldn't you have come into my life years ago?"

Returning the short swords to the box, she lay down on her couch and could not keep the tears from coming. Both Leather and Lace jumped onto the sofa with her and snuggled against their mistress. She cried harder.

~

Penny awoke to the chirping of her cell phone. She rubbed her eyes and the dogs jumped down. She snatched her phone and did not recognize the number on caller I.D.

"Hello," she mumbled.

"Merry Christmas, Pretty Penny."

She bolted up, wide awake. "Are you crazy? They'll find you!"

"I doubt it, but hearing your voice is worth the risk."

"Oh, shut up."

"Ah. I've missed that."

There was silence.

"Ninja Man, you there?" Penny asked.

"Yeah."

"You okay?"

"Lonely. I truly miss you. I'd become David Ulmer in a heartbeat if you could swing that."

"That would be a bit unorthodox and people would talk." Penny laughed. "I love my swords and my—um—flowers, not to mention the nunchucks and bo. Awesome."

"I love *you*."

"Stop before you get yourself dead."

"You could move here. You'd like it."

She sighed heavily into the phone. "I kinda wish."

"Can I call you?"

Putting the man off, she said, "I'm going to Laura Beth's for Christmas dinner. I need to get ready."

"Tell Little Momma I wish I could take it all back and I'm sorry."

"Tell her yourself."

Quiet followed before Marin said more urgently, "Can I call you?"

"Yeah."

"Merry Christmas, Pretty Penny. You just gave me the greatest gift."

"Merry Christmas, Ninja Man."

28
A Family Affair

Penny shivered in the biting wind and cold drizzle that was quickly becoming freezing rain. The door to the Copeland home opened, sending the aroma of cinnamon and nutmeg wafting onto the porch. The tall white-haired man, who opened the door, drooped one eye. "Sheriff Ulmer, right?"

"Yes, and you're Doug Blanchard, Madeleine's husband."

"Yes. Come on in. It's getting nasty. Laura Beth is in the kitchen." He pointed. "Want me to take that? What'd you bring?"

"Five dozen deviled eggs."

Doug took the large cardboard box. "Yeah, we might need that many. Laura Beth's family from Gulfport is here—her mom, dad, brother and sister-in-law with four kids. Bruce's mother and father and his sister with her two kids are here. Then Laura Beth invited the Montoyas who have the one little girl and the McGills, including Tanner's mother and stepfather and his two kiddos. She has Madeleine and me. You alone?"

They walked through the house which bustled with activity to the kitchen.

"Yep. By myself." A shadow passed over her face, and then she forced a smile.

Doug deposited the box and retreated to visit with the men. As she pulled pecan pies from the oven, Laura Beth waved to Penny and pointed to the wine. Penny poured herself a glass.

~

After the meal, Laura Beth disappeared to the nursery where she found her mother-in-law rocking Riker. The grandmother looked up. "He's growing so fast."

"Yes, he is. Is he asleep?"

"No, but he was fussing when I used the restroom."

"He's ready to nurse." Laura Beth reached for her son. In the other chair in the room she fed the baby.

Bruce's mother smiled. "He looks like Bruce."

Laura Beth nodded. "Then he'll grow up to be handsome."

The older woman laughed. "Yes, even if he was my son, Bruce was a good-looking man. So is Tanner McGill."

"What are you suggesting?" Laura Beth dipped one eyebrow.

"I see the way he looks at you."

"Momma Copeland, Bruce has not been dead a year. I can't believe you're insinuating that I'm doing anything with Tanner."

The older woman widened her eyes. "And why shouldn't you?"

"What?"

"Laura Beth, you'll always be my daughter and the mother of my grandchildren, but my son is dead. I would never expect you to mourn forever. You're young and beautiful. Are you attracted to Tanner? Do you have any sparks?"

"I like Tanner. He's a very nice man."

"Nice?"

"And funny and attentive." She sighed. "And very good-looking."

"And widowed like yourself and unattached to anyone." Mrs. Copeland smiled. "I could accept him as extended family."

Riker gave his mother a loud burp and she handed him back to his grandmother and sat back down. Mrs. Copeland began to rock the baby. Laura Beth asked barely above a whisper, "Are you telling me to stop mourning and to develop something with Tanner?"

The grandmother placed a kiss on Riker's head. "Honey, I want you to live. Tanner is a good man. I think you're attracted to him, and it's more than being grateful." She stood and placed the sleeping baby in his crib.

The two women stepped out into the hall. Freckles squeezed into the nursery and curled up under the baby's bed. Mrs. Copeland pointed at the dog. "That's what I'm talking about. When a man gives your children a pet, he wants to become family."

"Oh," Laura Beth murmured. "I'm not ready to marry again."

"That's okay. Take time to date. Get to know him and his family." She took Laura Beth's left hand. She tapped the wedding ring. "Put this away somewhere safe. Give it to Riker for his wife someday. It's time to move on."

They embraced. "Look at your two friends here," Mrs. Copeland continued. "Madeleine is my age, but she's found happiness with a man to fill her sunset years. Marge lost her husband. She's found something real with that Montoya fellow."

Laura Beth interrupted. "She was single for almost four years."

"Yes, but God has sent you Tanner sooner than that."

"You don't think it's too soon?"

Graying hair dipped to her left shoulder as Mrs. Copeland gave a half shrug. "Things are not as they once were. I'm not telling you to elope. Just give him a chance. This is a family affair. We're all in this together. Tanner fits with all of us. Bruce would not want you to be alone."

"I'll think about it."

"Don't think too long and miss your chance."

They walked into the living room with their arms around each other.

~

The Christmas guests trickled out. Those, who had longer drives, left first, fearing bad road conditions. Mrs. Copeland kissed her daughter-in-law's cheek. "Remember what I said." She nodded toward Tanner who was engaged in playing Uno with his two children and Laura Beth's two girls. "That is husband and father material. I approve."

Laura Beth's own mother gave her a hug. She looked after the woman who just left. "She's right."

"Did you two talk?"

"A little, but I'm not as likely to butt in as she is. This time, though, I agree with her. Love you, baby."

Marge and Luis left. He carried a sleeping Deannie in his arms. Marge whispered to Laura Beth, "My boss adores you. He's a good man."

"Is it a conspiracy?"

The blonde shrugged. "Could be. Thanks for having us."

Madeleine and Doug left. Madeleine smirked. Laura Beth held up a hand. "Don't tell me. You're in cahoots with my mother and mother-in-law."

"Nope, I just see how Tanner looks at you, and how you look at him without even being aware." Doug chuckled as he pulled his wife away.

He nodded at the young woman he had met as her census trainer. "We're giving Tanner's mom and step-dad a ride home. They rode over with Tanner but are ready to go; but Tanner's tied up, just like he wanted to be."

Penny followed closely behind the others. She stopped on the porch. "I'm not the last to leave. Ninja Man called me this morning. He sent me a gift. Laura Beth, a relationship with Tanner would *not* be complicated. Snag him or I will."

"Backstabber."

Penny laughed and hugged her hostess good night.

Laura Beth returned to the living room and sat on the floor beside Tanner as he started to deal a new hand of Uno cards. "Deal me in," she said.

"You have to take points the average of all ours," he said.

"Oh, bring it. I'll still win."

Tanner grinned. Corbin elbowed his sister and winked. His father cut him a look.

Laura Beth laughed out loud. "Let's play cards."

29
A Single Rose

After a late supper consisting of turkey sandwiches and some other leftovers from the feast earlier, Tanner herded his two children toward the car. He stopped in the doorway of Laura Beth's home. "Thanks for having us today."

"I enjoyed it. It took my mind off Bruce. Tanner"—She looked at the ground—"Tanner, you know I'll always love him, right?"

"Yeah." He lifted her face with his index fingertip under her chin. "Just like I'll always love my wife, but Laura Beth, you're a single rose. So am I, or I might be the thorn."

They both laughed.

Tanner continued, "Listen, I'd like to take you on a real date, not a friendly celebration, and then I'd like to take you to Gus's New Year's Eve shindig. If Madeleine and Doug can't babysit, my mom will gladly do it. How about early dinner tomorrow and maybe a movie? I can bring Mom here."

Laura Beth snickered. "So, the date would end when we walk in my door."

Tanner hooted with laughter. "Sugar, I'll take your kids to my house if you want. If you'd like the date to last all night, I'm game." A small stirring below his waist punctuated his willingness.

"Not just yet, but, yeah, okay. Dinner and a movie sound great, then New Year's Eve at Gus's. We can do a little line dancing." She grinned. "Do you dance?"

"Yes, ma'am. I'll be here, say five? We'll eat and catch a seven, seven-thirty movie. I'll have you home by ten. Does that work with Riker's schedule?"

"Yeah. I'm weaning him since I'm working. He's getting there."

"Good then. Until tomorrow. Night. Merry Christmas."

"Merry Christmas."

Tanner looked up. "Damn it! No mistletoe."

Laura Beth laughed. "Good night, Tanner." She gave him a playful shove out the door. Once the door closed, she sighed deeply. *I can see myself with Tanner.*

~

Roslyn McGill peeked in the open bathroom door where Tanner finished his grooming. "Hey, Dad! Wow, you're hot."

"Hot?" Her father chuckled. "Since when do you notice whether men are good-looking?"

"I'm growing up, Dad."

"Not too fast, okay?"

The girl nodded. "Are you gonna take Miss Laura Beth flowers?"

"Should I?"

"Oh, yes. All women like flowers."

"Then I'll stop and get some." He tweaked his daughter's nose. "Is Grammy here?"

"Yes, sir. She said to hurry up or you'll be late."

"I'm ready. It's casual dinner and a movie. Let's go."

Tanner made a quick stop at a florist on the way and returned with a single rose of variegated orange-white-yellow.

"Just one?" asked Roslyn.

"Yep. I don't want overkill. Maybe I can send more for Valentine's Day."

"Smooth move, Dad," said Corbin, and for the first time, Tanner noticed his son's voice broke just a little.

"Thanks for your seal of approval."

His mother laughed. "It is a good idea. Now we better go."

Tanner and his entourage arrived a couple of minutes before five. Laura Beth looked discreetly through her window. "Wow!" She mumbled. "He looks good. Those jeans fit well and that royal blue sweater over a pale blue oxford shows every muscle he has." Her stomach gave a flutter and the tingle moved a bit lower.

Stacey tugged her mother's hand. "You're talking to yourself, Mommy."

"Sorry. You open the door. I have to use the restroom really fast."

The little girl ran to open the door on the first chime. Laura Beth disappeared into her bedroom. She opened the bottom drawer of her standing jewelry box and pulled out a black velvet ring box. She twisted the one karat diamond engagement ring and wedding band inlaid with diamonds. Taking a deep breath, she pulled off the set.

Laura Beth swallowed hard. She whispered, "I'll always love you, Bruce Copeland." She kissed the rings and placed them in the box, putting it back into the drawer and closing it. *I will not cry. The time has come to move on.*

She finger-combed through her long auburn hair. The burnt orange cashmere turtleneck she wore brought out her skin tones and her brown eyes. Her jeans fit, and very little weight from her pregnancy remained. *New Year's resolution—Hit the tennis courts at least twice a week.*

She walked up front where the children were already picking out a home movie to watch. "Hey. Sorry, I had a quick stop to make."

"No problem." Tanner smiled. He presented the single rose.

Laura Beth took it and smelled the bloom. "Let me put this in a vase and we can go." She went to the kitchen.

Tanner touched his mother's shoulder. "Mom, she took off her wedding ring," he whispered in her ear.

"A good sign. She's a sweetheart. Go for it."

Laura Beth returned with the flower and placed it on the fireplace mantel. She looked at her girls. "You two be good."

"We will," they said together.

"Go have fun, Mommy," said Stacey. "You too, Mr. Tanner."

"I intend to," Tanner assured. He offered his arm to Laura Beth. "It's not nearly as cold as yesterday. Do you want a jacket?"

"I'll be fine." She kissed her daughters and waved as she went out the door.

In the car, Tanner said, "Is Casa Fiesta okay, or would you like something else? Then, I thought we could go see *True Grit*. I haven't seen it yet; have you?"

"Tanner." She laid a hand on his as he turned the ignition. "Relax. I love Mexican as long as I can have a margarita, and I've been dying to see *True Grit*. We've spent too much time together for you to be this nervous."

"Not as a real date."

She laughed. "Well, the single rose was the perfect opener."

"Thanks."

At the restaurant they shared the special house sampler, and both had two margaritas on happy hour. Then they went to the movie.

"Popcorn and a Coke?" Tanner asked.

She nodded. "With butter. And can we get Milk Duds?"

"Sounds good to me."

Tanner ordered the concessions and they entered the theater. Halfway through the movie, Tanner fumbled until he found Laura Beth's hand in the dark. She almost laughed at a very serious part of the film. *He's a nervous wreck. It's so cute.*

The movie over, they left holding hands. Tanner drove his date home. At the front door, he bent down to kiss her good night. The door burst open, "Dad! You have to come see this about a nine-year-old Boy Scout. It was so awesome!" Corbin gushed.

Tanner clenched his teeth. Laura Beth covered her mouth and laughed behind her hand. "Maybe next date, Detective."

30
My Ways Are Not Your Ways

Laura Beth tossed and turned that night as disconcerting dreams plagued her.

First, she dreamed about Bruce. The happiness she felt washed over her like a cleansing flood. Yet, though he was in her dream in a brightly lit expanse, she could not touch him. He smiled at her. "This is where I belong now, baby. I fought the good fight. I finished my race, even if it was shorter than I wanted it to be." He looked toward a golden road. "Baby, I kept a secret from you. I'm sorry. In a way, I'm glad my finish line changed from what I expected. Forgive the man you hold responsible. He did me a favor. Live. Love. You have so much love to give. Tanner is a good man. Tomorrow, call Dr. Jacobi in the Jackson office. He'll explain. I love you forever."

Like a mirage, he blended into the golden glow.

Laura Beth sat up and stared at the alarm clock. "It's just one?"

She lay back down and closed her eyes.

Sparkling blue water and a crystalline beach greeted her in her next dream. Tanner splashed in the sea, frolicking with the children while she spread a picnic. Nothing but joyous laughter echoed along the shore until she called the others to eat. The waves turned murky and pulled Tanner beneath them. Then, a giant wave grasped Corbin and dragged him down. Tanner bobbed back up, searching frantically for his son. "Sugar! Help me he called."

Try as she might she could not get to the desperate man.

She bolted upright in her bed.

"Dear God! What is going on? Was there too much butter on the popcorn?"

Again, she looked at her clock. "Two."

She got up and went to the bathroom, where she searched the medicine cabinet for a bottle of melatonin and took one pill when she found it.

Back in bed, she curled up, almost afraid to sleep.

The pitch-black ocean billowed and tossed Tanner on shore. A furtive shadow with a big nose battled the waves to get to where Corbin was last seen.

Katana flailing, the shadow chopped tentacles off a monstrous octopus. With the final swing, the creature hurled the boy onto the beach.

"I'm sorry," shadow said. "I swear I didn't mean to, and as God is my witness, I will protect you and yours from this day forward."

Laura Beth screamed when she sat up this time. She saw dawn approaching. "I'm not going back to sleep."

She pulled her daily devotional from the bedside table, along with her Bible. The book fell open as if guided to Hebrews 11:1. In the early morning light Laura Beth read, "Now faith is confidence in what we hope for and assurance about what we do not see."

~

About ten the next morning, Laura Beth's phone rang. She scowled when she saw the number—Dr. Jacobi. Her heart raced. She answered.

"Laura Beth?" the older doctor who had been Bruce's mentor asked.

"Yes."

"I've been meaning to visit, but things have been crazy without Bruce. His patients are having to come to Jackson."

"I dreamed Bruce told me to call you last night."

"But you didn't."

"No."

"You should have."

"What was his secret?"

"He didn't tell you?"

"No."

The older man sighed. "Laura Beth, Bruce had stage four pancreatic cancer."

"What?" she screeched.

"There was nothing to be done. He didn't want to tell you until after the baby came. He thought it would stress you too much. He wanted to continue as normal until he couldn't. Maybe it's better he went quick."

She rubbed her face. "Oh, my God."

"I'm sorry."

"It's okay. But I had some crazy dreams last night. The others still don't make sense. Thanks for calling."

~

Laura Beth secluded herself in her bedroom for a while. She tried to pray, but her thoughts were jumbled. She breathed out, "Why? And what does 'Ninja Man' have to do with this? Or Tanner and his son?"

A soft voice came to her. "My ways are not your ways. Know that because of Bruce many will be saved—even the man you want to hate."

31
Midnight Mess

In spite of her disturbing dreams and news, Laura Beth anticipated the New Year's Eve date with Tanner. She dragged Penny to Jackson to go shopping with her to find the perfect outfit to wear. Penny laughed. "Wish I had a date. I'll be at midnight mass."

"Penny, I'm nervous. He almost kissed me the other night. I really hope he *does* for New Year's."

"Well," said the sheriff, thumbing through a rack of sequined tops, "you'll be at Gus's. Great fun, but it's not the country club or a fine dining establishment."

She held up a three-piece outfit of brown satin with a brown silk blouse, the jacket and slacks having a metallic gold pinstripe. The legs flared and it was a four petite. "This would go so well with your coloring."

Laura Beth took it. "I found this ecru linen with heavy brocade on the lapels. It is so you."

"Why do I need something like that?"

"Why not? You can wear it to mass."

Both ladies tried on the garments and bought them. "Shoes," said Laura Beth. "We need shoes."

Laura Beth found a pair of four-inch heels that matched the brown perfectly. She looked at Penny. The sheriff shook her head. "I don't need heels. I'm almost six feet as it is. What about these winter-white flats?" She held up a pair of slipper-looking shoes.

"They would look good with that outfit."

Shoes chosen, Laura Beth pranced to the jewelry department of the large department store. She chose gold chandelier earrings and a bangle for her wrist. "I'd say you're set," Penny said.

"You need jewelry."

"Why?"

"Just because." Laura Beth picked out a pair of diamond posts. "I know you don't go for flashy, but these are classically elegant. You're beautiful, Penny. *You* need to believe that whether a man says it or not."

"Thanks."

~

Madeleine picked up Laura Beth's children at seven. They would be staying the night at the older woman's house. Laura Beth did a little twirl in her new clothes. "Nice," said Madeleine. "Did you get some lingerie?"

"No!" Her face burned. "Why would I do that?"

"What if he stays the night?"

"Madeleine, I am not ready for *that*. This is only our second *official* date. All I want is a New Year's Eve kiss. More would just be a midnight mess right now. I'm not saying that I wouldn't consider more with Tanner—just not yet." Bruce's dream words came back to her.

"Suit yourself, but don't hurry to pick up the kids. Remember I'm cooking the traditional New Year's Day meal. Bring Tanner and his lot with you."

"You shameless hussy! I'll see if he wants to come."

"I already invited them."

Madeleine took the children, and Laura Beth put the final touches on her makeup. "Not bad," she said to her reflection as her doorbell rang.

Having found a little bit of his dog voice, Freckles barked in a way Laura Beth had never seen. She rubbed the puppy's head. "It's okay. I'm expecting Tanner. He's a few minutes early, but we can have a drink or something."

Laura Beth opened the door to find a tall man wearing black jeans, a black button-down shirt, black cowboy boots, a black Stetson and a black trench coat. His very short coal-black hair gleamed in the bright moonlight. "Shit!" she exclaimed and started to close the door.

"Wait!" the man said, holding up his hands as if in surrender.

"Marin, is that you? You don't look the same."

"So, you didn't recognize me, Little Momma? I had a nose job and a little chin taken off. Better?"

"You expect chit-chat? *Forgive the man you hold responsible.* "What the hell do you want? How did you get here?"

"I'm Ninja Man, remember? I'm not here to hurt you. I have something for you and the children."

He reached inside the trench coat and felt cold steel at the back of his head. "I can pull the trigger now," Tanner said.

"I heard you drive up, and I didn't run."

Tanner spun Marin around. Tanner's eyes grew wide. "New look?"

"Yes."

"Well, you might change your wardrobe. It's a dead give-away." Tanner still held the gun in Marin's face. "Thought you died in a plane crash. I knew that was too good to be true."

"Lower the weapon. I'm not here to hurt anyone." He glanced over his shoulder. "I'm not armed."

"What do you have in the coat?" asked Tanner.

Carefully, Marin pulled out a large manila envelope and handed it to Laura Beth. "I can't apologize enough. I know this isn't much, but it's a gift to help with your kids. Maybe one day you can forgive me."

Laura Beth opened the thick package with tentative fingers. Inside were documents giving each child five shares in Puro Petróleo. The logo for the company was Marin's intricately entwined serpents. "For their education," Marin said. "It's legal. I do own the company, just not under my given name, as you can see by the signature." He laughed a second. "Did you know that I don't really even know what my given name is? The nuns named me."

"Enrique de la Vega?" Laura Beth still looked perplexed. "Tanner, I think you can lower the gun." He did so with reluctance. She looked back at the man who might have killed her. "When do you go back to Argentina?"

"As soon as I talk to Pretty Penny."

"Do you hope to talk her into going with you? Are you still on the government's payroll?"

"I hope so, and I can't tell you."

"Shit," muttered Tanner. "You're still doing covert ops."

Marin shrugged. "What would you two do if Pretty Penny agreed to marry me?"

"What?" they cried in unison.

"I know I wouldn't be your first choice for her, but I'm nuts about her."

"Penny de le Vega?" Laura Beth echoed. "Sounds off."

"Well, I have another name for this country, and she wouldn't have to change her name unless she wanted to."

"You want me to look at your sorry ass every day after what you did?" Laura Beth arched an eyebrow. *Forgive the man...*

"Well, my ass looks a bit worse after what *you* did." He made a thin line with his lips. "You shot me in the ass, Little Momma. You almost killed me.".

"I could have gone straight for the heart, but I wanted you to suffer. Besides, I wasn't sure you even had one."

"And I deserved that." He dipped his head in one affirmative nod. "Look, I love my villa, but I'm lonesome. I can swing it so I'm there most of the time as Enrique de la Vega, but I'd like to come here some and be with Penny, if I can convince her. Here, I'd be David Black. And, yes, I'm still working, but I get to call my own shots now. I only take assignments that I think *truly* need to be eliminated. I'd love to take out a few Al Qaeda and more than a few Mexican drug cartel leaders. I'll also be doing extractions. This is who I am. I can't change that. I don't know how to be anything else. I've been on Uncle Sam's payroll since I was eighteen. I'm forty. During that time, I've done some things you'd consider heartless, but I've also done things you'd call heroic. I've earned a college degree in forensic science and I've trained more than one assassin. Just call me Jason Bourne if you'd like."

He took a step away from Laura Beth. "I'm going now. If you do research, McGill, you'll find Diego Marin has never existed. I'm a ghost, a shadow. At the very least, I died in a fiery plane crash."

Tanner almost lifted his sidearm again. Laura Beth touched his hand. "No. It's time to move on. Mr. de la Vega, thank you for the generous gift. If you want to see Penny Ulmer, she'll be at midnight mass. We only have one small Catholic church."

She placed the documents on a table inside the door. "We have a date, Tanner. Let's go."

The man in black disappeared into an equally dark car and drove away. Tanner's expression was unfathomable.

"Would you be able to live with that prick nearby?"

"I don't want to see the mess he might make at midnight mass, but Penny has a thing for him." She dipped her head to her ear. "It'll be all right. He might come in handy someday." She sighed. "I had a dream where he was actually a real-life hero. And God told me His ways are not my ways."

~

Penny walked into the church, genuflected and made the sign of the cross. She slid onto the back pew. She was a little late, having almost stayed home. The priest had already begun the homily. After a short time, the congregation was asked to kneel and pray.

A susurrus to her right, made the sheriff open one eye. A man clad in total black knelt, made the sign of the cross and slipped in beside her. He got so close, his hand brushed hers.

As the parishioners began to recite responses to the priest, the man said, "I almost missed you."

"Shit!" She turned her head toward the voice. "What did you do to yourself? Why are you here?"

"Take me home, Pretty Penny. I'll tell you everything."

The two rose as the man of God pronounced the benediction.

~

In the church parking lot, the sheriff demanded, "You tell me everything right now, and I mean now. Start with the new face." She circled with her index finger close to his face.

He tapped his nose. "Rhinoplasty." He touched his chin. "I had them take a bit off here too." He had left the hat in the car for entering the church. He swiped a hand across his head. "Chopped off all my hair. Do you like it? I think I look nicer, less intimidating." He grinned, showing perfect white teeth.

"What are you doing here?"

"Bringing in the New Year with you."

"You're gonna get killed."

"Naa. I'll be okay. I need to talk to you anyway."

"I said you could call me, remember? *Phone* me. "

"No. I'm gonna say this once, so listen up. I'm just outside Buenos Aries. I'm living as an oil mogul named Enrique de la Vega. I'll continue that cover. I'm still working for a secret organization, but I get to take only the jobs I want. I already talked to Little Momma and McGill. Penny, I want to be here part of the time. I've already worked it out to stay here as David Black. Hernandez is no longer a threat to me, I've been assured. I love you, Penny. I know I'm despicable, but I really do have a good heart. I want to marry you. I won't be able to stay here all the time. I have to go back and forth to South America. You can come with me all the time there or just some of the time. I don't care. I just want to be with you."

Penny started to speak. He held up a hand. "Let me finish, please."

She nodded. He went on. "You might want to punch me, but I looked into your past. I know about the lieutenant colonel. If you want me to make an example of him, I will. One thing I have *never* done is rape a woman. I understand why you try to be such a badass, but you are the perfect woman for me. You are my Pretty Penny."

The bells in the church belfry began the chime to ring in the New Year. Marin pulled Penny to him. Without waiting for her to push away, he kissed her soundly.

She responded in kind. Her heart raced and she felt lightheaded.

Breaking the kiss, he said, "Take me home, Pretty Penny."

"I'll get my car tomorrow. I can't drive right now."

~

Two huge canines greeted Penny and her guest. He took a step back. "You'd better meet them," she said.

She patted each dog's head. "This is Leather. Pet him."

Marin rubbed the black Great Dane's head.

Penny smiled. "This is Lace."

He gave the tawny dog a ruffle on its head. "And who should I tell them you are?" the sheriff asked. "Which name would you like to use?"

"I'm David Black, your daddy, if your momma will agree." He dipped his head toward the animals.

"David," she repeated. "I'll have to get used to it."

"Will it be hard?" he asked with a lopsided smile that showed a single dimple.

"Oh, shut up." She took his hand. "Ask me in the morning."

What sounded like a hungry growl came from Marin's throat. He pulled her into his arms. He gripped her hair tightly on both sides of her head and kissed her with a burning passion.

Penny pushed him back and slid the trench coat off his arms onto the floor. Her hands gave the front of David's shirt a yank, sending buttons in all directions. She ran her hands up his taut chest. "You have the best body I have ever seen." A scar on his right side just below his pectoral muscle caught her attention. She rubbed her thumb across it.

"Purple heart," he said in a husky whisper.

He kissed her again, hard. His tongue danced with hers. She found the button of his jeans and unfastened them. She slipped her hand inside, finding what it sought—his already erect penis. Back and forth, she ran her hand the full length of his pulsating shaft. Both of them groaned.

David kissed her neck and took off her blazer then her blouse. He unsnapped her bra and let it drop to the floor. His mouth moved to her breasts. His tongue flicked across her right nipple as he rolled the left one between his thumb and index finger. "Oh, mmm," Penny panted when he caught her areola in a firm suck then gentle nibble. She pressed his head to her chest.

He opened the button on her slacks. They joined the mound of clothes that was accumulating. He trailed kisses and nips down her stomach. Getting to the top of her pelvic bone, he slipped the silk panties she wore down. When the undergarment reached her ankles, he flipped her shoes off and tossed them over his shoulder and then the panties joined the shoes. He knelt and lifted Penny's right leg to his shoulder.

She let out a squeal with the first brush of his tongue across the soft folds of her labia, and then as he increased pressure and depth, teasing with his tongue, barely slipping one finger inside her. Agonizing minutes of longing ignited blazing passion. Penny moaned as the heat spread over her. She grasped his hair in her hands. "Oh, my God!" She pulled him to his feet.

He stepped out of his boots as Penny wiggled his jeans down. He took a step back and looked at the woman before him. "You taste sweeter than I could have imagined," he said. "Caramel and honey do not compare."

Hands on her waist, he lifted her into the air, and she wrapped her legs around him. The consuming desire left no time to find the bedroom. David pressed Penny against the wall, and he was inside her. His perfect rhythm increased intensity. She met his every thrust and clutched his buns, urging him deeper. "Yes! Yes!" Penny screamed with abandon.

Two dogs whined, unsure if their mistress was in distress. "Harder," she said and bit into David's shoulder.

Muffled thumps echoed off the wall. "Oh, yeah! Pretty Penny!" David yelled as he exploded. Penny shivered, every cell of her body feeling as if an electrical current were shooting through her.

David buried his face in the crook of her neck. "Happy New Year, Pretty Penny," he mumbled against her skin.

"Happy New Year, David Black. Yes, I'll marry you."

31
Slow and Easy

Gus's Goulash was ablaze with lights and music. Parking was hard to find. The proprietor's reputation for throwing a New Year's Eve bash had spread to other towns and many partygoers' car tags showed they travelled as many as a hundred miles. Gus had resorted to selling tickets and adding space on the patio area that was usually only used in warmer months by having a fire pit put in. Tanner had gotten two tickets before Thanksgiving with the hope that Laura Beth would go with him.

Alcohol flowed liberally at the party, but Gus had employed a number of the high school kids and college students, home for the holidays, to act as designated drivers. Fifty dollars for the night, free food and soft drinks was good pay for fun to boot, and some folks tipped generously when taken home safely. Clyde Dixon, a senior at Sunrise High School, appeared to be the take-charge underage participant. Laura Beth and Tanner greeted the young man who had once saved her life.

"Keys," he said.

Tanner shook his head. "I won't be drinking much. Maybe a beer and a glass of champagne at midnight, but you keep up the good work because not everybody will do that."

Tanner steered his date toward the dance floor. "Happy New Year," she called over her shoulder to her one-time rescuer.

The laughter and fun intensified with each drink a person consumed. Laura Beth had a lemon drop martini. "Whoa!" she said. "Stout, but good." Tanner had a Coke.

Finished with her drink, the couple joined a line dance in progress. Then a Texas two-step started up. After that a bit of free style dancing brought both Tanner and Laura Beth back to their table and another round of drinks, Tanner with a frosty Guinness on tap and Laura Beth with a crisp pear martini. She licked her lips. "Oh, this one's really good."

"Good thing I'm driving." Tanner smirked. "Slow and easy, Sugar. You wouldn't want me to take advantage of you in an inebriated state."

"Maybe I would." She flirted and batted her lashes.

He lifted an eyebrow.

"Okay, I wouldn't," she admitted.

"Finish that drink and let's dance some more. It's got to be getting close to midnight."

They finished their drinks and moved back to the dance floor where the music had slowed, and the dances had become more intimate. "Easy" by the Commodores wafted from the jukebox.

Sudden silence brought everyone to attention. Gus's servers busily passed out glasses of champagne. He started the countdown. At the stroke of midnight, the patrons drank their toast and deposited glasses wherever they could find a spot. Tanner spun Laura Beth around after she set her glass down. He cupped her face in his hands and kissed her with a deep, passionate kiss. She moved into his embrace as his hands slid down her arms and around to the small of her back. Her arms moved around his neck as heat pooled in bodily regions that had not been touched in some time.

"Happy New Year, Sugar," Tanner whispered against the lobe of her ear as another slow dance began.

"Happy New Year, Cream."

"Cream Puff."

~

Tanner escorted Laura Beth to her front door. He stopped on the porch, his breath leaving frosty mist as he spoke. "Good night."

She tipped her head to the side. "You want to stay?"

He took a step back, eyes wide.

She shook her head. "Not for sex. I'm nowhere nearly ready for that step. I need to take things slow and easy, but I wouldn't mind sleeping in your arms."

"Okay. Let's watch a little bit of the Times Square celebration before we turn in, and I'd love some hot chocolate."

"Sounds good."

Laura Beth made cocoa for both of them and brought it to the sofa. Tanner flipped on the television, took a sip of hot chocolate, and spewed it across the room. "Holy shit!"

Laura Beth screamed, "Call Penny! Now!"

Tanner dug his phone out of his pocket and dialed the sheriff. She answered dreamily, "This had best be an emergency, Tanner McGill. You can wish me a Happy New Year later."

"Turn on your TV. You have to see the breaking news. Have you seen Marin?"

"He's right here beside me. What's wrong?"

"Turn on the TV. I don't think it'll much matter which channel."

Penny's new lover sat up beside her. "What's wrong?"

She pointed to her remote on the nightstand. "Turn on the TV."

Both law enforcers and their dates watched intently as every network broadcast breaking news:

> *Undersecretary of State Margarita Hernandez was facing indictments on a number of charges. Authorities say the scene was gruesome. Apparently, she was killed earlier this evening. Confirmation has been received that*

the woman was decapitated with a very sharp blade. There was no evidence of hacking and it would seem the deed was done with a single blow. There was no sign of forced entry, so speculation is that she knew her assassin.

In a related story, at bed-check time this evening at the federal prison in Leavenworth, Kansas, the body of Hernandez's cousin, Carlos Perez was discovered, also without his head attached...

"Marin's there?" Tanner asked for clarification. "He was here four hours ago. There's no way he could have been in both Texas and Kansas and gotten here that fast."

"It's his signature mark." Penny looked at the man beside her.

"Pretty Penny, how could I be three places at once?" Tanner heard the question in the background. "You know, I'm not the only person the government employs."

"Penny," Tanner said, "even if he did this and somehow made it look as if it happened while he was here, will any of us lose sleep over that vile woman's death? Or that despicable bastard's?"

Laura Beth gripped Tanner's thigh.

"No," came out loud and clear over the phone. "Now, good night, Tanner. Happy New Year. I have other men I'd rather be talking—or not talking—with." The phone clicked in his ear.

He laid the phone on the table. "Sugar, are you upset?"

Laura Beth shook her head. "Nope. I just wanted to be sure Penny was okay."

"Sounded more than okay." He smirked.

"Yeah. Don't get ideas. Let's go to bed."

A couple of miles through the woods, Penny Ulmer took "David's" face in her hands. "You did it. I know you did. I don't want details, but this is the arrangement you made. Someone higher up the food chain wanted them dead."

"Pretty Penny,"—He ran a finger along her jaw line—"My katana is on my dojo wall. This I swear to you."

She tilted her head to the side. "Don't lie to me. This would be an assignment you'd want. If you can't tell me *where* you're going, I'll understand, but always tell me you *are* going."

David sighed and dropped his hand onto the down comforter. "Very well. As God is my witness, I did not kill either Perez or Hernandez, as much as I would have enjoyed that—especially Hernandez. I usually have worked alone, but not always. There was once a team. McCormick was once a part of that team before he went rabid. There were others who shall remain nameless, but know this—the organization is international. Someone very political wanted to save face. I cannot specify by name. Some old friends made it happen. Are you going to shed tears?"

"Hell, no!" She covered his mouth with hers.

~

Laura Beth stretched and yawned. The aroma of coffee made her open her eyes. Tanner held a cup out to her.

"You entered my kitchen without permission?" she teased.

"Yes, ma'am. And I let Freckles out. That was the right thing to do, wasn't it?"

"Yes." She took her coffee and sipped before she laughed. "I wonder what he'll bring up today."

"He brings you gifts?"

"Oh, yes. Several squirrels, an old sock, a piece of knotted rope, and a kid's tennis shoe. Where he found that is beyond me."

They heard pawing and whining at the door. Tanner shook his head. "I'll have to install a doggie door and train him better."

She got out of bed and held her hand out to the man sitting on the side of her bed. "Let's let him in."

Walking to the door, they heard a thump on the porch. Laura Beth raised an eyebrow. "It's heavy," she stated.

"A limb?"

She shrugged and opened the door.

Penny probably heard Laura Beth's scream at her home through the woods. "A limb, Tanner? Was that supposed to be a joke? That's a human leg!"

Word Count 50,240 (54,558) (56,168) (56,392) (57,637) Final—

(57,957)

About the Author

Like many of her characters, Janet is a history buff and loves anything of historical significance from old cars to old cemeteries. Get to know Janet and you'll see why she's been critically acclaimed at the Faulkner Wisdom Competition and why her writing continues to receive 4 and 5-star reviews, as well as winning awards—It could be that readers see so much of her in her characters: mother, educator, author, editor, native Mississippian, graduate of the University of Southern Mississippi and Belhaven University, and a person who has overcome great obstacles and still holds on to her faith.

http://www.janettaylorperry.com/
http://janettaylor-perry.blogspot.com/
https://authorcentral.amazon.com/gp/profile
https://www.facebook.com/Author-Janet-Taylor-Perry-299698950061301/
janettaylorperry@gmail.com
https://www.facebook.com/janettaylorperrybooks/
Instagram: @janettaylorperry & @jtaylorperry
Twitter: Janet Taylor-Perry— @mom5kidz421
Goodreads:
https://www.goodreads.com/author/show/7376480.Janet_Taylor_Perry
Pinterest: https://www.pinterest.com/mumzy25/
YouTube: https://bit.ly/30hJsYg

Laura Beth and Tanner will be back in…

Bone Dry

Laura Beth Copeland draws human body parts like sugar draws ants. Finally safe from her encounter with a serial killer who decapitated his victims, she tries to put her life back on track. Detective Tanner McGill is intent on being in her life. As a romantic gesture, he gives her children a Pitbull puppy they name Freckles.

After a New Year's kiss from Tanner and his staying the night, their peace is shattered when Freckles brings his mistress a gift. Tanner jokes that it sounds big enough to be a limb—But he never dreamed it would be a *human* limb. Freckles delivers a human femur, and the body count mounts once again. And again, those Laura Beth loves are put in grave danger.